THE ACCIDENTAL GENIUS OF WEASEL HIGH

RICK DETORIE

EGMONT
USA
NEW YORK

EGMONT

We bring stories to life

First published in the United States of America by Egmont USA, 2011
443 Park Avenue South, Suite 806
New York, NY 10016

Copyright © Rick Detorie, 2011
All rights reserved

1 3 5 7 9 8 6 4 2

www.egmontusa.com

Library of Congress Cataloging-in-Publication Data is available

ISBN 978-1-60684-149-5
eBook ISBN 978-1-60684-244-7

Book design by Whitney Manger

Printed in the United States of America

CPSIA tracking label information:
Printed in March 2011 at Berryville Graphics, Berryville, Virginia

This book is dedicated to all those educators who are passionate about teaching, and in particular to Michael Iampieri, who fueled my interest in the creative arts and has been a constant source of inspiration since that very first day of Art Class 1-A at Loyola High School so many years ago.

Thanks:
Dan,
Greg,
Mary Ann,
Joe,
Mike,
Tom,
Ned,
Joann,
Gen,
Terry,
Sandy,
Claire,
Andrew,
Louie,
Steve,
Doug,
and
Jennifer.

FOREWORD

On the first day back to school after winter break, Mr. Hawley, freshman English teacher at Arthur C. Weatzle High School (commonly known as Weasel High), distributed spiral-bound notebooks to each of his students in his returning freshman class. He told the class that because he was unhappy with the overall poor writing skills and penmanship many of them exhibited in their work last semester, he was starting off the New Year with a long-term assignment that would run twenty weeks, from January through May.

The assignment required that each student maintain a personal blog, a notebook blog.

At least once a week, in their own handwriting, each student was to post an entry of any length. A post could be a couple of sentences, or multiple pages. Over the course of the assignment, Mr. Hawley would be periodically checking on each student's progress.

In the notebook blog, bloggers would be expressing their original thoughts and ideas. If their brains contained no original thoughts or ideas, they could write about other people's thoughts or ideas. They could write about things they'd done and places they'd been, people they know, TV programs they watch. They could write about pets, sports, cars, music, fashion, anything.

Students were to refrain from using texting abbreviations and profanity. They were also forbidden to use the word *suck* in any of its variations or connotations.

The notebook blog would count for one-third of their final grade. However, the blogger with the most compelling, interesting, or humorous blog—as determined by Mr. Hawley—would receive the special grand prize of a sum total grade of 100 for the semester.

What follows is the notebook blog of student Larkin Pace, who won the grand prize.

THE DEFINITION OF AN ACCIDENTAL GENIUS

An accidental genius is somebody who possesses an awesome talent that happens to be totally useless.

It's like the guy who can solve the Rubik's Cube in ten seconds, or the girl who can multiply huge rows of numbers in her head and come up with the right answer every time.

And then there's me, who's seen, like a million movies in my life (my dad teaches a film course and brings home tons of DVDs), and if you name any movie I've ever seen, I can tell you the plot, the cast, the director, the studio, and the year it was released.

And that's not all. I can even recall entire scenes and repeat, word for word, big chunks of dialogue. But because most people find it really annoying when I do that, it's a superpower that I tend to keep hidden.

Most of the time.

— LARKIN PACE

TEN THINGS I HATE ABOUT BEING 14

My mom has to drive me everywhere.

I never have any money.

Even girls are taller than me.

My sister Kelly (no matter what age I am).

Zits.

I can't think of five more right now. I'll have to finish the list later.

BROOKE

Yesterday afternoon, Brooke and I went to the mall to hang out.

Hanging out is pretty much all we can do at the mall, since neither of us has enough money to actually buy anything.

In the window of the electronics store I saw my dream camcorder. When I have enough money saved, I'll probably buy it off the Internet, but seeing it in person is truly a beautiful experience.

I pressed my face against the glass and shouted.

I had really been hoping to get that camcorder for Christmas—you know, under the tree—but no such luck.

Brooke is totally cool. I've known her since third grade when we played each end of a rainbow in our class play, "The Monkey Puzzle Tree." I had really wanted to play Bob, the lead monkey, but Ms. Holzinger gave the part to Joey Bernucci. I personally think it was because, of all the kids in our class, he was the hairiest.

Since the rainbow thing, Brooke and I have been very close. We do a lot of stuff together and tell each other everything. She's been my girlfriend for so long that we even think alike.

We spent most of the morning at the mall Larkin Snarkin'. That's what Brooke calls it, but she's actually a lot better at it than me.

Snarkin', I mean. You know, watching people, then making snarky comments about them.

That "We are becoming aggravated" line is from *Matrix Reloaded*. Brooke is almost as good as I am at remembering lines from movies. She can't repeat all the dialogue from an entire scene the way I can, but she's good at recalling the corniest lines. Brooke's sort of an Accidental Genius in training.

Later we scraped up enough change to split a sub for lunch.

While waiting for our order, we did a few lines from the movie *Scarface*.

16

Yes, Brooke is awesome.

The thing I especially like about Brooke is that she's easy to talk to. I can kid around with her, and she gets most of my jokes, even the lame ones. We laugh at most of the same things.

When you try to kid around with most girls, they take everything personally and get all offended. And they say things like, "What's that supposed to mean?" and "Is that supposed to be funny?"

Oh, give me a break.

Okay, maybe I do have a hard time talking to girls I don't know very well, but it's not because I'm shy or anything. It's just that they're hard to figure out.

Okay, so maybe I am kind of shy around girls.

So Brooke and I spent the rest of the day at the mall walking around and making each other laugh.

What could be better than that?

RANCHO DE LOS REJECTS

The barking woke me up. The clock said 5:18 A.M.

I knew the Buddies had to be barking for a good reason. Either a fox or a raccoon was looking for a free chicken dinner.

Sure enough, out on the roof of the chicken coop sat a big fat raccoon fiddling with the fence.

I ran outside, tossed a stone at it, and just missed. The raccoon turned and gave me one of those "Is that all you've got, dude?" looks. So I opened the kennel gate and let the dogs out.

All sixteen dogs (all named Buddy because many of them came without names, but they all answer to Buddy) took off after the raccoon, who jumped off the roof and disappeared into the darkness.

Then, as I do every morning, I slid open the squeaky barn door and fed, watered, and cleaned up after the turkey, nine cats, five rabbits, seven hamsters, and Troy and Vanessa, the potbellied pigs who live there.

Where did all these animals come from?

The city and the suburbs.

What typically happens is that people buy their kids a baby chick or a bunny for Easter, or a puppy or a kitten for whatever, and sooner or later, those cute baby animals grow up. And they become messy and noisy and farty, and the family decides to find them a new home somewhere, usually the woods.

But it just so happens that our place is the last farm before the woods. So people looking to dump their unwanted pets figure: "Why not leave them on a farm instead? That clueless old farmer probably has so many critters running around on his farm, he won't even notice one more."

Wrong.

We do notice them. And we take good care of them.

And we're not farmers.

We don't grow any crops and we moved into this place with only one nonhuman, our dog Buddy.

Make that two nonhumans, if you count my sister Kelly.

19

You see, my mom and dad bought this place as a "nonworking" farm, but let me tell you, for a nonworking farm, there sure is a lot of work to be done around here.

Anyhow, after the Buddies returned (raccoonless, as usual), I fed them and headed back to the house, where Dad was making coffee. He was already dressed in his professor clothes. You know, a real tie (not a clip-on) and shiny black shoes. And pants, of course.

His full name is Martin Aldo Pace Junior, and he teaches English literature at the college and a class called Classic American Cinema. That means movies. Old movies. Many of them are in black and white and most of the people in them are dead. I mean, they're dead now, not back when they made the movies.

My dad brings home tons of DVDs, so I've watched maybe a thousand movies, and I can remember everything about them, including huge stretches of dialogue. I have some kind of total recall, but it only seems to work with movies, and not with history or math or anything that might be useful to me in school.

So while he wasn't awake enough to be thinking too clearly, I told my dad about the camcorder at the mall and asked him if he'd let me get a work permit to get a job so I could earn the money to buy it.

But he said:

Then he told me he'd speak to my mom about me working part-time for her or something.

Yeah, whatever.

MY EIGHTH BIRTHDAY

I remember four things about the day I turned eight.

Grandmom Pace said my long hair made me look like a girl. So, on the morning of my party, without my parents knowing about it, she took me to her hair salon to get it cut. Before they cut it, though, a girl named Kristi washed my hair in a shiny black sink. She was the shampoo girl, and she was very gentle and didn't let any water get into my eyes or ears. Kristi was the most beautiful woman I had ever seen.

During the party at the pizza place, Freddie Schnase got a dry-roasted peanut stuck up his nose, and the paramedics came and took it out. Then we had to hurry and cut the cake because the next party was coming in at two o'clock.

When we got home, my mom and dad gave me my best present ever: a 6.0-megapixel optical-zoom digital camera. It was my first grown-up toy.

Later that night I stood in front of the closet mirror and tried to imagine what I would be like in ten years.

I was pretty sure I'd look a lot different: bigger, taller, and older looking. But I wondered, would I still be the same me?

Would I still be into Legos, Transformers, and cookie-dough ice cream? Would I still want to be a professional soccer player? Would I still like to hike in the woods with my dogs and watch old movies with my dad?

And would my sister Kelly still be a total monster?

Well, yesterday I checked myself out in the mirror again, and it's sad to report that not much about me has changed physically. I'm only four years away from being eighteen, but I don't seem to have gotten any bigger.

I don't play with kids' toys anymore and I don't want to be a soccer player.

Now I want to be a film director, like Martin Scorsese or Steven Spielberg or Jason Reitman.

Some things that haven't changed: I still like cookie-dough ice cream, hiking with my dogs, and watching old movies with my dad.

I still have that same dinky little 6.0-megapixel camera.

And my sister Kelly is still a total monster, only now she's twice the size.

TEN THINGS THAT BUG ME ABOUT MY DAD

10. He's always correcting my grammar.

9. He's anti-video games. He says video games make you fat and lazy.

8. He's no fun anymore. It seems like not so long ago, we used to go out and do stuff together. Not lately, though. I guess because he's old.

7. He's old.

6. He doesn't laugh when I say something funny. He'll tell me it's funny, but that's about it.

5. He brings home tons of movies, but won't go with me to see any of the current popular ones.

4. He never plays catch with me, or football, or basketball, so I can't do any of those sports. All he ever does is ride his bike dressed up in weird bike shorts and a weird helmet, which makes him look like the monster from the *Alien* movies.

3. He drives too slowly. He even lets old people in hats pass us.

2. Whenever we go someplace and they give him back too much change or an extra order of fries by mistake, he returns it.

1. He won't set me up with a professional-quality camcorder so I can get started in my career as a director.

HOW I GOT STUCK WITH LARKIN

My mom's name before she married my dad was Diane Larkin.

That's right. I got her old name when she dropped it for Pace. My mom liked the name Pace because it's Italian for "peace."

Sometimes my mom gets all Italian on us, but that's cool.

As for me, I never had a problem being named Larkin until middle school. That's when all the usual losers started making fun of it.

Yeah, I've heard them all.

Oh, and one more thing about my name.

I've been friends with Freddie Schnase since we were in preschool. We've gone on vacations together. We were in Cub Scouts together. We've had sleepovers at each other's houses. We have lunch together nearly every day. We're closer than most brothers are to each other.

But recently I've come to realize that I've never heard Freddie say my name. Larkin. Maybe he says it to other people when I'm not around. I don't know, but I'm pretty sure I haven't heard him say my name to ME.

From now on, when I'm with Freddie, I'm going to start listening for my name. He'll have to say it sooner or later, right?

My mom said I ought to just talk to him about it, but she doesn't realize that even when Freddie and I do have a conversation, we don't really talk about anything.

MY MOM

Yesterday afternoon, while I was watching this week's recordings of *The Price Is Right* and, of course, taking notes, my mom came in to tell me something.

She said she'd had a discussion with my dad about me wanting to earn extra money to buy a camcorder, and the possibility of me working part-time for her, and, well, she had some good news.

One of her regular clients, an older lady named Mrs. Grubnik, would like someone to come to her house once a week to do light chores. The job paid ten bucks an hour, which would work out to about thirty per week.

"Hmmm," I said, "are we talking about a mysterious old lady who perhaps lives in a creepy old house? And might those chores include hosting séances, changing her mummy's bandages, and tossing raw meat to the creature in the cellar?"

"I don't think so," said my mom. "The chores are probably more along the lines of vacuuming, changing lightbulbs, shoveling snow—that sort of stuff."

"Oh. I guess I might be able to do it," I said, trying not to sound too disappointed.

"How about Wednesday afternoons?" she asked. "You could take the bus to her house after school, and I'll pick you up from there at about six."

It took me about half a second to think it over and agree to do it. Then I said, "Do I need to take anything with me?"

She paused at the door and said, "Well, because you never know what you might find in an old house like that . . ."

Whoa, is my mom cool or what?

She's always kidding around, but she's real subtle about it, you know?

I don't think my mom was always cool, or funny.

Back when she was in college, she was a very serious artist and dancer. She studied something called batik, which is a fancy way of dyeing fabric with wax. It used to be popular with hippies and other people who are too cheap to put real art on their walls.

But what my mom really loved to do was dance. She was real good at something called Modern Interpretive Dance. It's sort of like ballet, but more jiggly.

Then, when she married my dad, who's a lot older than her, and they bought this farm, she stayed home to raise Kelly and me. But it's not like she gave up this terrific dance career or anything.

One time, when I thought it would be a good idea for her to get out of the house for a while, I checked the Help Wanted ads, but the only dancing jobs available around here involved poles and laps, if you know what I mean.

After she took a carpentry class, she started building stuff for us, and eventually, for the neighbors, too. So now she's a professional handyman. She drives a pickup, wears overalls, and is into power tools.

On Career Day at my old school, while the other parents told us all about their jobs as law clerks and party planners, my mom brought in a chain saw and fired it up in the classroom.

The mask was my idea.

ENTER THE BEAST

This morning, after finishing all my chores in the chicken coop, the kennel, and the barn, I invaded the kitchen with a fierce kind of hunger.

It's too bad that nothing worth eating was anywhere to be found. Sure, the cupboard was filled with all kinds of cereal, but not one of them was frosted, chocolate-flavored, marshmallowy, or even close to being "magically delicious." Instead there was a lot of "high fiber" stuff that, between you and me, looks, smells, and tastes like critter kibble. Trust me, I know.

Then in stomped Kelly, who plopped her backpack on the chair by the door. Mom was right behind her.

"Kelly, have you had breakfast yet?" asked my mom.

"Yes, Mother," said Kelly. "I had some ibuprofen."

Kelly was sporting her new look this morning. Lately she's been wearing a plastic thing under her hair that makes it look like there's a little speed bump on top of her head. I think she ordered it from an infomercial.

As they left the room, I heard my mom say, "Now, Kelly, breakfast is the most important ..."

I checked in the refrigerator, and miracle of miracles, in the freezer was one solitary fudge bar. It was left over from last night. And it was Kelly's.

Hey, I had no choice.

I was hungry, and, as you heard: "Breakfast is the most important something or other," so I started to remove the wrapper, and:

Or she'll what?

She has no power over me. Not now. Not anymore.

Although, I do admit, she *used* to, and I mean BIG-TIME.

When we were little, my big sister Kelly was a total thug. She once held me down and threatened to let loose a giant loogie on my face if I didn't submit to being her slave.

And so I was her slave for a while, and did all the usual things that three-year-old slaves do, like:

But the worst thing she ever did to me was make me dress up in a bunny costume to help her sell lemonade at the front gate of our farm.

I was too young to remember it, but if I *could* remember it, I'm pretty sure I'd never forget it.

"Or you'll do what," I asked her, "make me wear a hot, itchy bunny suit on the side of the highway in the middle of August?"

"I'll tell Mom you let the dogs in the house the weekend she and Daddy went to New York," she said.

"Big deal," I said. "I shampooed the carpets afterwards, and besides, that's ancient history."

"Oh, yeah?" said Kelly. "Was it ancient history last week, when I saw you hitchhiking home from school?"

Uh-oh, busted.

Now she had me.

Never mind that it was freezing cold and I had a ton of stuff to carry and it was a little old lady driving and it was just that one time. It would kill my mom if she found out.

So I gave in to Kelly's threat and gently returned the fudge bar to the freezer, giving it a little good-bye kiss.

As soon as she left the room, I sprang into action. I removed the fudge bar from the freezer, tore off a corner of the wrapper, and tiptoed over to her backpack. I unzipped the back pouch, dropped the fudge bar inside, and re-zipped it.

Mission accomplished.

Later that evening, when Kelly got home from school, she was so mad she was foaming at the mouth, and it was all because the fudge bar in the backpack had melted into a sticky mess all over her learner's permit. Just as I had planned.

She had a big slobbery meltdown and said, "There's a big bucket of angry eyeballs hanging over my head and each one is telling me that my life is a disaster in the making!"

"Talking eyeballs?" I said.

Then she ran crying upstairs and slammed her bedroom door so hard that a picture frame in the hallway fell off the wall and broke, and now I have to pay to replace it.

$10.99 plus tax!

There goes my monthly budget.

But you want to know something?

It was totally worth it.

LUNCH WITH FREDDIE

I was in the cafeteria having lunch with Freddie, and as usual, we weren't talking much because we hardly ever do. So I asked him what kind of cracker sandwich his mom made for him today, and he said, "Pickle."

Let me explain something here.

When he said pickle, that doesn't mean his cracker sandwich has sliced pickles between two crackers. What it does mean is that his mom squirted pickle juice on crackers and put the crackers between two slices of bread. That's what they call a cracker sandwich at the Schnase house. Sometimes Mrs. Schnase puts ketchup or mustard or butter on the crackers. She once tried honey, but it made everything too gooey.

Freddie's family does a lot of weird stuff like that.

His mom once saw a chef on TV bake some bread in clay flowerpots, so she tried it. She made the dough, put it into a flowerpot, baked it in the oven, and served it to Freddie and his dad for dinner. But the problem was, she'd used an old flowerpot that wasn't clean and still had dirt and old roots and stuff in it. His dad got mad and yelled at her, and ever since then the only thing she cooks is Lean Cuisine.

Another thing his mom does is wash her car in her pajamas. Every Saturday morning, if the weather's nice, Mrs. Schnase can be seen in the driveway, soaping up the Subaru in her pj's and fuzzy slippers.

Freddie likes to wear his pajamas a lot, too, but only in the house and under a bathrobe. Lately, though, he's been wearing his bedroom slippers outdoors, and even to school. He says it's because they're comfortable, and there's nothing in the dress code that says he can't wear them.

He also wears baggy pants, but not saggin' like the other guys. He wears them way up high with a belt, like some old guy who's wandered away from the rest home.

If Freddie keeps dressing like that, he's never going to get a girl-friend. Unless, I guess, she's kind of weird like him. They'd never be able to go out to a nice restaurant, because Freddie will only eat at places where he can watch them fix his food. That way, he says, he makes sure they don't spit on it or mess with it in any way.

So anyway, Freddie and I were in the cafeteria having lunch when I spotted Dalton Cooke across the room. He was going from table to table, eating food off other people's trays.

I took out my camera and started filming it.

"Why are you doing that?" mumbled Freddie.

"Because it's right out of *The Miracle Worker*," I told him.

"Remember that scene when Patty Duke as, you know, Helen Keller, went around the table and was eating whatever she wanted off her family's plates?"

"I don't know what you're talking about."

"Freddie, *The Miracle Worker*, 1962, directed by Arthur Penn, it's a classic! Remember that scene where Patty Duke first realizes the sign for water?"

Freddie looked at me like I was crazy or something, so I acted out the scene for him.

"You mean you've never seen *The Miracle Worker*?" I asked him.

"No," said Freddie, "and why would I want to see a movie about people who eat other people's food?"

By then, Dalton was at our table.

He poked his finger into my chicken taco and sneered.

Then he picked up a portion of Freddie's cracker sandwich, examined it, grinned at Freddie, and took a big bite.

Whoa! I thought his eyes were going to roll back into his head. He made a choking sound and spit Freddie's sandwich onto the floor.

"What's in that thing, used toilet paper?"

"That's right, Dalton," I said as he staggered off. "Why don't you come back tomorrow? We're having dog-hair burritos!"

"No, we're not," said Freddie, all serious like. "Tomorrow's Saturday."

MEET THE NEW BOSS

My mom picked me up at school on Wednesday and took me to meet the lady I was going to be working for: Mrs. Grubnik.

41

She seemed like a nice old lady, especially when she was talking to my mom and calling her "Diane, dear" and telling her not to worry about a thing, because she and I would get along just fine. Stuff like that.

But as soon as my mom left, she turned to me and said, "I'll have none of your nonsense around here. Do we understand each other, young man?"

"Yeah, sure," I said. "Yes, ma'am." Though I wasn't sure what particular nonsense of mine she was referring to.

Then I started thinking maybe she's like Santa Claus or the CIA, and has spies following me around.

Her house didn't seem haunted, but it looked old and smelled old. Kind of like gravy. And it was quiet. Real quiet. I didn't see a radio or a TV anywhere, and there were no animals in the house. The place really needed a dog.

She led me through the house and explained what my chores would be.

In the room she called the sunroom was her "art collection." She has about a million tiny statues of weird-looking chubby people with big heads who are dressed like the kids in *The Sound of Music*.

She called them figurines and said they were off-limits to me. I was not to touch them.

"They're collectables," she said. "Do you know what 'collectable' means?"

"Sure," I said, looking around the room. "A collectable is something that collects a whole lot of dust."

I don't think she appreciated that remark.

The first thing she had me do was replace the burned-out bulbs in her chandelier. The whole time I was doing it, she stood next to the ladder and kept yelling, "What you break comes out of your pay! Remember that, Mister Smarty-Pants!"

After that, she had me replace the plastic hooks on her shower curtain.

Then it was time to clean out the hall closet.

Mrs. Grubnik said it was her intention to empty out the entire closet and give everything that was in it to charity.

Yeah, well, it didn't exactly work out that way.

Every single item I pulled out of the closet, she had me put back in, "because," she said, "it's something I'll probably need sooner or later." We're talking about stuff like six umbrellas, three pairs of rubber galoshes, a ukulele, a pith helmet, a box of incense, a pink plastic walrus, an Elmer Fudd mask, a 1967 telephone directory.

Okay, that I *did* convince her to toss.

43

At one point a framed photo fell off the top shelf, and I caught it just before it hit the floor.

"Be careful!" she shrieked. "Do you know who that is?"

I wiped the dust off the glass, thinking it was probably a picture of Mr. Grubnik, but I saw right away that it wasn't.

"It's William Holden," I said.

"*You* know who William Holden was?"

"Sure," I said, "he was a big Hollywood star, one of the greats. He was in *Bridge on the River Kwai, Stalag 17, Sunset Boulevard . . .*"

Then I looked straight at her and said, "You're Nora Desmond! You used to be big."

Mrs. Grubnik's eyes opened up real wide, and she said:

She was real impressed and wanted to know how I knew lines from an old movie like *Sunset Boulevard*. So I told her my life story: how my dad teaches an American cinema class and how he brings home lots of movies—new and old—and how I've seen most of them and can remember tons of dialogue.

I also told her that I'm going to be a movie director one day, and my girlfriend Brooke is going to star in my first feature film.

Mrs. Grubnik and I spent the rest of my time there talking about old movies.

She told me she remembers the first movie she ever saw, *Too Hot to Handle*, the one with Clark Gable and Myrna Loy.

She said she's always loved movies and that seeing a favorite movie you haven't seen in a while is like visiting with an old friend, only better, "because a movie will never tell you you're looking old, or ask to borrow money for new dentures."

You know, for a mean old lady, she's pretty cool.

SIZE MATTERS

I was having a math test today and needed my lucky shirt, but I couldn't find it.

It's an old shirt that I bought at the beach. It says: "Oh, yeah? The voices in my head are telling me I'm *not* crazy!" I know it's kind of lame, but that shirt's gotten me through tests, quizzes, and even an oral report called "Dental Hygiene for Dogs," which featured a slideshow of me brushing and flossing one of the Buddies' teeth.

Well, I finally found it in a pile of dirty clothes in the laundry room.

While there, I checked my height against the measurements on the door frame to see if I'd grown any since last week, which was the last time I'd checked.

No change.

I'm beginning to worry that I'm never going to grow. My dad said that he didn't get his first real growth spurt until he was eighteen, but I'm worried I might *never* get a growth spurt.

I'm afraid I might take after my mom's side of the family or, worse, one day I might find out I was adopted, and my real parents are tiny circus people.

It's something I worry about.

I THOUGHT YOU WERE HER

Brooke's mom dropped us off at Meadowbrook Ice-Skating Rink for the afternoon. The plan was that we were going to take the bus home. The bus goes right by Brooke's house, but I have to take the bus all the way to Post Road, then walk another mile back to the farm.

Brooke's a pretty good skater and she has her own skates. I'm a really bad skater and I have to rent.

After I got my skates from Hector, the skate-rental guy, and sat down to lace them up, a lady in a baseball cap started asking Hector a lot of questions. The main thing she wanted to know was Meadowbrook's policy on "crack the whip."

I was never a part of one, but I remember when I was a little kid and used to watch the big kids form whips on the ice. That's when everybody joins hands and skates around in a big circle, faster and faster until the person on the end loses control and crashes into the wall. Awesome.

"No, ma'am," said Hector to the lady in the baseball cap, "that's not allowed here at Meadowbrook anymore."

"Good!" said the lady. "Because it's a dangerous practice that encourages violence and antisocial behavior. If you allow those whips, before you know it, fights will start breaking out, or even worse, a hockey game!"

"Actually, ma'am," said Hector, "we have hockey games here every Tuesday and Wednesday."

"Well, that proves my point exactly," said the lady.

It wasn't too crowded on the ice. Brooke did her fancy moves out in the center, while I hugged the wall and gave the evil eye to any little kid who skated better than me—which happened to be all of them.

I eventually let go of the wall and managed to skate along with the crowd and not kill anybody. Or worse, embarrass myself.

In fact, I was doing pretty well until the "Ghostbusters" song started playing. About half of the skaters let out a cheer, while the other half scrambled to get off the ice.

The reason I didn't want to skate during "Ghostbusters" is because every time the word *ghost* is said in the song, everybody on the ice has to immediately turn around and skate in the opposite direction. That's not easy for me to do, because I have trouble making sharp turns.

I also don't know how to stop. My technique for stopping is to slam into the wall or skate into another person, preferably someone large and soft.

Luckily, Brooke took me by the arm and spun me around with each "ghost," that popped up, and we made it through the entire song with only one or two minor collisions.

The next song was a waltz, and this old guy named Russell, a Meadowbrook regular, skated out to the center and did his Regular Russell stuff: spins, axels, camels, you name it. When he finished he skated off, acting all proud of himself, and some people applauded.

I was about to take a break, when Brooke skated over to me and said all excitedly, "Larkin, do you recognize the song that's playing?" I did.

That's right, it was the theme from *Titanic*.

She dragged me out to the center of the rink. I wasn't too happy about it, but then I decided, *Hey, why not? Let's go for it.*

I said, "Smell ice, can you?" in a very loud voice.

We continued doing one scene after another from the movie until the final scene.

"You must do me this honor," I said. "Rose, promise me you'll survive. Promise me now, no matter what happens."

By that time we were holding on to Brooke's scarf and she was circling around me like I was a carnival ride or something.

"I promise, Jack," she said.

"Never let go, Rose," I said.

But before Brooke could say the last line, a very loud voice shouted: "Whip! Whip! No whips allowed! Call security!"

It was the lady in the baseball cap.

I let go of the scarf, and Brooke fell backwards and plopped onto the ice. We both looked at each other and laughed. Then we clumsily got to our feet and made our way to the bleachers.

A couple of people cheered, and some applauded, but I couldn't tell if we'd gotten a bigger hand than Regular Russell. I'm pretty sure that we did, even when you take into account that most of the people were clapping with gloves on, so it wasn't that easy to hear.

After all, *we* were the bigger hot dogs.

We went to the café and split a hot chocolate, using spoons to sip it, then headed out to the bus stop.

It was pretty cold and the wind was blowing, so we huddled together real close. It felt good.

We were talking about everything, then Brooke started saying how different high school was from middle school, and how she'd made a lot of new friends and all. Then she said, "And how about you, Larkin? Have you found a girlfriend yet?"

At first I thought she was joking, and I smiled at her, but the look on her face said she was dead serious.

All of a sudden, I couldn't breathe. It was like somebody had kicked me in the gut.

All this time I'd thought *she* was my girlfriend, and I was her boyfriend. We're together all the time. We've known each other since forever. We share our secrets, our ambitions, our dreams, even our hot chocolate!

I had big plans for the two of us. I'm not exactly sure what they were, but I do know they were *big*.

It was too much to think about, so I sort of shut down.

The bus came, and we got on, but I don't think I said anything during the entire bus ride. I don't even remember Brooke getting off at her stop, or saying good-bye to her.

During the walk home I kept thinking about how stupid I'd been.

Then I thought about all the things I should have said to her when she asked me if I'd found a girlfriend yet.

"Yeah, baby, and I'm lookin' right at her."

Or "There's only one you, there's only one me, and there's only one we. Got it?"

Or I'd give her a sexy kiss that's so long and passionate she gets all dizzy and almost passes out. Then I'd look deep into her eyes and say in a husky, manly voice: "What do *you* think, baby?" Then I'd wipe my mouth on my sleeve and walk away.

When I got home, I went straight to the kennel to hang out with the Buddies. I might not know much about girls, but there is one thing I know for sure about dogs. They always know exactly who you are to them.

And one more thing.

I want to add this to my list of "Ten Things I Hate about Being 14." When you're fourteen, and somebody you really like stabs you in the heart, you don't know what to say.

I don't think grown-ups have this problem.

At least not in the movies.

FIVE THINGS I HATE ABOUT P.E.

1. Dalton Cooke

2. Dalton Cooke

3. Dalton Cooke

4. Dalton Cooke

5. Dalton Cooke

GETTING PHYSICAL

It was raining today, so P.E. was inside the gym.

When it rains, we usually play basketball for twenty minutes then run laps around the gym floor until somebody passes out.

The first thing Coach Pierson did was yell at Freddie for wearing bedroom slippers and make him put on the old gym shoes Freddie keeps in his backpack for such emergencies.

We divided up into four teams and played two half-court games. Coach Pierson was so bored that he sat in his office for twenty minutes, then came out and blew his whistle for laps.

He yelled at us to "Keep it moving! Keep it moving!" Then as soon as he returned to his office, we stopped all that moving.

When he blew the final whistle and yelled, "Hit the showers," we headed for the locker room.

I didn't sweat too much from all that non-moving, so I decided to skip the shower. While I was getting dressed, I heard a big commotion around the corner.

There, some of Dalton's guys were holding down Freddie and it looked like they were trying to force somebody's tighty whiteys over Freddie's head, sort of like an underpants ski mask. Except there was nothing whitey about these tighties, if you know what I mean.

I went over and tried to break it up by saying, "Hey, come on, you guys," and Dalton Cooke said:

I did not want to be next, so I went back to my locker, got my stuff, and headed out. A blast of cold rain hit my face, and I decided to turn around and do the right thing.

I went to Coach Pierson's office.

He was seated at his desk studying something on his laptop, and it didn't look like game schedules. You know?

"Coach Pierson," I said. "Dalton and his guys are harassing a guy in the locker room."

"Oh, yeah?" he said without looking up from his laptop. It was obvious he didn't care.

So I said, "They're harassing a minority student."

That got his attention fast. He lurched out of his seat and out the door.

I snuck a peek at what was on his laptop, then I left.

And it's not like I lied to the coach. I mean, if a guy who wears bedroom slippers to school isn't a minority, I don't know who is.

Later, at lunch, neither Freddie nor I said a word about how I'd rescued him.

And I did rescue him.

I'm not saying I saved his life, but if you've got a pair of dirty, smelly underpants on your head, you're liable to come down with a bad case of jock itch on your face.

Or worse.

I'LL HOOK YOU UP

The last time I was at Mrs. Grubnik's house, I found out that she does have a TV—two of them, in fact. One is a portable that's upstairs in her bedroom and has a converter and rabbit ears. It gets four channels.

The other one is in her living room. The reason I didn't see it before is because it's in its own cabinet and the cabinet door was closed. It's real old and doesn't have a converter, so it doesn't get any channels.

She also has a DVD player that's still in its box under a table in the sunroom. Her son Richard gave it to her three years ago.

Mrs. Grubnik has a problem with Richard. She told me that on Thanksgiving she makes him sit at the kids' table.

That's because she really, really hates Richard's ex-wife, Angie, and Richard has "Angie" tattooed on the back of both of his hands. Mrs. Grubnik says that if she has to see that horrible woman's name every time Richard passes the candied yams or Brussels sprouts, she'll get indigestion. So it's better that he sit with the little kids, since most of them can't read anyway.

My chore today was to hook up the DVD player to the big TV in the living room so that Mrs. Grubnik could watch a DVD I'd brought her.

But there was a problem. There was no place for the DVD cable to plug into the back of the TV. There was a piece missing, an attachment or something.

I explained the problem to Mrs. Grubnik and offered to get the part at Radio Hut, an electronics store that's a couple of blocks from Mrs. Grubnik's house.

"How much do you think it'll cost?" she asked.

"I don't know." I shrugged. "Ten, twenty, maybe thirty dollars."

"Okay, I'll be right back," she said.

She went briefly into the dining room, then returned and handed me a small patch of tightly folded bills. It was warm, which made me think she probably pulled them out of her bra.

Ick! Not only was it old-lady warm, it was old-lady-*bra* warm. I quickly put the money in my pocket.

"There are two twenties there," she said. "If you need more, come back and I'll give you more."

There was nobody in the store except a big guy at the counter who was reading a text on his phone. His lips were moving as he read.

I explained my situation, and he told me I needed an RF Modulator and showed me where they were.

The cheapest one they had was $24.99. I knew I could probably get a cheaper one online, but that would take too long, so I said, "I'll take this one."

He handed me a clipboard with rows of names and stuff on it and told me to write down my name, phone number, and e-mail address.

Just what I need, I thought, *more voice messages and spam.* So I wrote down somebody else's name and info.

"That comes to a total of $37.74," he said.

"Huh?" I said. "That seems like a lot. I thought it cost $24.99."

"Yes, plus tax, and ten dollars for the five-year limited warranty."

"I don't want a warranty."

"You said you wanted the five-year warranty," he said.

"I did not, and I don't want it!"

"Too late," he said, "I already rang it up."

Then this short lady came from somewhere in back and said, "What's the problem here?"

"I don't want the warranty," I told her.

"But I don't want it," I said, trying my best to make my voice sound sort of manly, "and I'm not paying for it." But it came out sounding sort of squeaky.

"I already rang it up, Mommy," said the big guy.

"You shut up!" she yelled. "If he no want warranty, it *his* problem!"

She picked up the clipboard, looked at it, and said to me: "You be very, very sorry you no get warranty, Mister Kelly Pace. Big-time sorry!"

So they deducted ten dollars from the bill.

And I wasn't a bit sorry.

However, I'd like to add one more item to my list of Ten Things I Hate about Being 14: People think that just because you're fourteen, you're stupid, and therefore they can take advantage of you.

Back at Mrs. Grubnik's, I hooked up the DVD player to the TV, and we watched *Some Like It Hot*, the DVD I'd brought with me. I was pretty sure Mrs. Grubnik would like it for two reasons: One, it's a classic, and Two, because for some reason, old people think it's funny when men dress up like women.

I don't know why. They just do.

THE LOVE DANCE

I was riding with my mom downtown in her pickup, and she was talking about something, fish fillets or caterpillars or something like that, but I wasn't paying attention because I was thinking about Brooke.

Then my mom said, "Larkin, look!"

There, standing in the doorway of an empty store was an old lady. She was holding a long cardboard tube like a batter at home plate. A lefty batter.

Pretty soon, a man walking along the sidewalk passed by her, and as he did, she leapt out, swatted him on the butt with the cardboard tube, and shouted: "Twenty-six!"

The poor guy tore off down the street.

"Should we wait around and watch her catch number twenty-seven?" my mom asked.

Oh, NO, I thought, why hadn't I brought my camera with me? This would've made an awesome little video.

It's all Brooke's fault for making me so forgetful.

"No, why bother?" I said, feeling all angry at Brooke.

And so we drove off.

After riding in silence for a while, I decided to ask my mom about me and Brooke, but I didn't want her to think it was about me and Brooke.

"Mom, can I ask you a question?"

"Sure, honey, anything."

"Okay, so I have this friend, see? And he, like, has this girlfriend he's been seeing for a really long time, but they never talk about their relationship or anything. Then one day, his girlfriend asks him if he's found a girlfriend yet."

"Oh, dear," said my mom.

"Yeah, I *know!*" I said. "Should he be, like, worried?"

"Well, it seems to me that she doesn't think of him as her boyfriend, and maybe that's her way of telling him that she's interested in another guy."

Oh, no, I hadn't thought of that.

"But," continued my mom, "chances are if they're very young, and they really love each other, there's always the possibility they'll get back together again someday."

"How can you tell if two people are really in love?" I asked.

"Oh, there are lots of ways. For example, look at that couple over there. You can tell by the way they're walking together that they're in love."

There was this guy and a girl walking and talking and moving around each other almost like they were dancing.

I thought real hard, and tried to remember if Brooke and I had ever done a love dance.

I wasn't sure.

DALTON COOKE

I was standing in front of the school, waiting for my mom to pick me up, when all of a sudden, a sharp whack on the back sent me staggering forwards.

It was Dalton Cooke, of course. His signature "slap" on the back is his way of letting you know who's boss.

"Hey, Pace Man, you're just the guy I wanted to see," he said. "I got a little project for you."

I try my best to avoid Dalton.

Even though he's a freshman, he's a couple of years older than the rest of us because he had to repeat the first and fifth grades.

We were in the same elementary school, but never in the same class. I mostly ran into him on the playground.

Then, when his parents got divorced, and Dalton burned down the garage, he got sent to one of those Thank-You-Sir-May-I-Have-Another schools. When he returned:

Then, when Dalton's dad married Dalton's stepmom, Dalton shaved the cat, and he was forced to go to therapy for a year, where:

So anyway, he started telling me about this stunt he and some other guys had pulled at the boarding school he'd attended, and he planned to do it again here, and he wanted me to be a part of it.

It goes something like this: Dalton's posse would collect about fifty backpacks and hook them together to create an enormous chain. Then they'd strap some guy (me!) in the bottom backpack, and lower him off the roof of the three-story building.

"But why me?" I asked him. "Why not *you*?"

"Because we need somebody puny who doesn't weigh a lot. We'd get a girl to do it, but it's probably against the law or something, so you're the next best thing."

Oh great, so I'm the next best thing to being a girl.

"I don't know," I said. "It sounds pretty dangerous. What if I fall and break my back or something?"

"What are you, a wuss? Now you're even starting to *sound* like a girl. Man up, dude!"

Just then, Dalton's stepmom drove up and blasted the car horn. "Listen, you think about it," said Dalton. "I'll get back to you later."

He tried to smack me on the back again, but I ducked, lost my balance, and tumbled face-forwards onto the sidewalk.

ERRRRR

Why is it, I thought, *that the biggest jerks have all the luck?* Dalton has it made: all the girls in school want him, and he has a hot stepmother and a totally cool dad.

His stepmom, Darbi, has actually appeared in a store catalog in her underwear, which I keep under my bed—the catalog, not the underwear.

She also gets paid to lean against cars and have her picture taken with old guys at the auto show.

His dad, Jack Cooke, used to coach our soccer team for half a season, and I'm not sure what he does for a living, but he's rich. He buys Dalton anything he wants: motorbikes, jet skis, and three ATVs.

And that brand-new sports car his stepmom had just driven up in? It's Dalton's as soon as he gets his driver's license.

Compare that to a dad I know, who won't even *lend* his kid the money to buy one basic camcorder to help his son get a jump-start in the career he's been dreaming of since Day One.

And that's all I'm going to say about that.

For now, anyway.

SHE WHO MUST GET HER WAY

It was another typical evening at the Pace home.

I was on the couch in the den, fast-forwarding through that morning's *Price Is Right* and taking notes. My mom was at the desk searching for recipes in her cookbook. My dad was in the next room grading papers.

Suddenly, there was a huge crash, and the house shook like it had been struck by a meteor. And into the room burst Kelly.

"My life is ruined!" She sobbed. "It's just one big rotting whale carcass on the beach of broken dreams!"

That was a new one, and not a bad one, at that.

My mom handed her a box of tissues. "What's wrong, Kelly?"

"R-R-Robby M-M-Markowski," said Kelly, her voice cracking with emotion, "isn't t-t-taking m-m-me to the junior d-d-dance."

Then she blew her nose so hard, the tissue flew across the room and landed on my knee.

"Oh," said my mom, "I didn't know that you and Robby had agreed to go together."

"Well, we never actually talked about it. But I've been real nice to him lately, so I just assumed he'd ask me."

Robby Markowski? Let me tell you what a loser Robby Markowski is. Last summer he got caught boosting a Hannah Montana coloring book at the dollar store.

"But he asked Amber Toppler instead!" wailed Kelly.

"Hey," I said, pointing to the tissue perched on my knee, "are you going to do something about this?"

"Don't you torment me, Larkin!" she shouted. "Make him stop, Daddy, please."

My dad was standing in the doorway. "Larkin, stop tormenting your sister," he said.

"I'm tormenting *her*?" I said. "She's the one who dropped the booger bomb on my leg."

Kelly moved over to my dad and rested her head against his chest.

"Now, now, princess, it's not the end of the world," he said.

"Thank you, Daddy, that's very comforting." She looked up at him and continued, "I feel so much better now, thank you."

Watch out, here it comes . . .

"Do you know what would make me feel a whole lot better?" she said. "If I could have my bedroom completely redecorated."

"Kelly, we just did it six months ago," said my mom.

"I know, mother, but that was *so* last year!"

"No to that," said my mom.

"Okay, then," said Kelly, "how about a kitty? I'd so love to have a cat, and I promise I'll take good care of it. Cross my heart."

"Now, Kelly," said my mom, "you know about your father's allergies."

"But what if I kept it only in my room?"

By that time, I'd had enough. I flicked the booger bomb off my knee, put on my headphones, cranked up the music, and watched as the three of them played out the entire scene. Wordlessly.

I later found out that they'd decided to let Kelly have one of the barn cats, and it would be restricted to her room. The cat would enter and exit her room, which is on the second floor, by way of a ramp which my mom would build on the outside of the house.

And guess who gets to help her build it?

That's right: yours truly.

TEN THINGS THAT BUG ME ABOUT MY SISTER

10. She goes ballistic whenever I touch her stuff.

9. She leaves the stuff I'm not supposed to touch everywhere.

8. She borrows my stuff without ever asking.

7. She rolls her eyes at everything I say.

6. She and her friends giggle whenever I pass by.

5. She pasted little heart stickers all over my skateboard.

4. She put lime gelatin in my favorite shoes.

3. She posts dorky pictures of me on the Web and forwards them to her friends.

2. She always gets her way.

1. Actually, everything about her bugs me. Seriously.

THE COWARDLY LION

I miss Brooke.

We haven't hung out together since the ice-skating incident. Sure, I've run into her at school a few times, but I didn't know what to say to her, so we wound up saying, "Hi! How are you? Good."

I'd called her a few times but didn't leave a message because I didn't know what to say.

"Hi! How are you? Good."

Yesterday I was looking for some batteries for my camera, when I came across a picture of me and Brooke in the third grade when we played the rainbow in our class play.

The one thing that really sticks in my mind about the play was the scene where Joey Bernucci and the other monkeys found the magic key and were about to unlock The Box of Ultimate Happiness. At that very suspenseful moment, Brooke coughed, and I yelled across the stage:

Yeah, sure, I knew you're only supposed to say "Bless you" when somebody *sneezes*, but she was so cute, I had to say something.

Anyway, the audience thought it was pretty funny.

I thought about phoning Brooke to tell her that I'd found the rainbow picture, but that seemed like a pretty lame reason to call.

No, I needed to come up with something that would really get her going and make her laugh.

And then it hit me.

I remembered reading somewhere that when he was ten years old, actor Robert De Niro played the Cowardly Lion in his school play *The Wizard of Oz*.

Brooke knows who Robert De Niro is, and everybody knows his famous line from *Taxi Driver*, so I decided to tell her about my idea for a video.

I called her home phone instead of her cell.

Her mom answered.

"Hi, Mrs. Wallace, is Brooke there? This is Larkin."

"Oh, hi, Larkin. Just a minute."

She sounded real friendly, even though I'm pretty sure Brooke had told her the news: "Guess what, Mom? Larkin Pace thought I was his girlfriend, and he was serious! Can you imagine such a thing?"

Then they probably had a big laugh, and Brooke's mother probably made some pot stickers, sort of Chinese dumplings, because for a non-Chinese lady she makes the best pot stickers in the world, and they probably ate them and spent the rest of the evening talking about what a dork I am for thinking Brooke was my girlfriend.

I suddenly felt kind of sad, because I realized that I would never again have any of Brooke's mom's pot stickers. It was all very sad. Bordering on tragic, really.

"Hi, Larkin," said Brooke.

"Hi, Brooke," I said, "I've been meaning to call you."

"Oh?" she said.

I took her pause to mean she wanted *me* to say something next.

"Uh, yeah, you know Robert De Niro, don't you?"

That didn't sound right, so I tried to explain what I meant.

"I don't mean *know* him know him, not like he's a friend of the family or an uncle on your father's side, not that he couldn't be an uncle on your *mother's* side, too. I've met all of your relatives, except for the cousin who lives in Cincinnati and has one green eye and one blue one, and in my opinion, they're both really good. The sides, I mean, not the eyes. Though I bet the eyes are probably good, too."

I was really messing things up. That didn't even make sense to me, and I'm the one who said it.

"Hold on, Larkin," said Brooke. "I've got another call."

I could hear her cell phone ringing in the background.

"Hello?" I heard her say, "Oh, hi!" Her voice suddenly got all smooth and sexy. "Nothing. What are *you* doing?"

She was talking to a guy! I could tell!

"Larkin," she said to me, "I have to take this call. Talk to you later, okay?"

"Okay," I said, and I clicked off.

This was bad. Really bad.

THE AMY FORDYCE PROJECT

Last night I lay awake and rehearsed what I was going to say to Amy Fordyce today. I planned on asking her to go with me to Friday night's basketball game.

I had decided that if Brooke was going to be dating other people, then so would I. Two could play at this game.

Actually, four, if you count Brooke, her date, and my date and me.

And Amy seemed like a good choice. She's smart, she's good looking, and she's not that much taller than me.

My problem is that I have trouble talking to girls I don't know too well.

I'm okay at first, as long as I've planned out what I'm going to say. But after the conversation gets going, my mind starts to wander and I tend to lose focus, mainly because I'm thinking stuff like:

But I decided to do my best and play it cool when I saw her after health class today.

Why did she have to ask me a question I didn't know how to answer?

Crash and burn!

TO MARKET, TO MARKET

I was out in the yard raking leaves, while Miss Sadie was inside asleep on the couch watching the movie *The Big Sleep*.

It's been "Miss Sadie" ever since last week when Mrs. Grubnik told me to call her Sadie. I did at first, but it felt weird to call an old lady by her first name, so I settled on Miss Sadie.

Hey, Larkin, you might ask, *why are you raking leaves in March? Didn't those leaves fall off the trees last November?*

That's because, according to Miss Sadie, it's pointless to rake leaves in the fall, because over the next few months, they're going to blow into your neighbor's yard anyway.

So I was raking her neighbor's leaves.

After I'd finished raking, Miss Sadie asked me to go to Big Al's Market to buy a few groceries she needed. She gave me some money, a list of what she wanted, and had me take a rusted old wagon that she kept under the back porch.

I asked her why she didn't get one of those two-wheeled carts that people take to the store, and she said, "Those things are death traps! If you get a bunch of old people together, wheeling those wiry things this way and that way, you'll be lucky to get out alive."

"Oh," I said.

At the store I found everything on her list, and got into the "Ten Items or Less" line.

Then this happened:

I'd like to add one more thing to the "Ten Things I Hate about Being 14" list: Grown-up ladies with big bosoms are kind of scary.

A KITTY FOR KELLY

On Saturday morning, my mom and I put the finishing touches on Kelly's cat ramp.

It was awesome, if I do say so myself.

The ramp extended up the side of the back porch to the porch roof, then to Kelly's bedroom window, where mom had installed a cat door.

I asked Mom if we were going to paint it, but she said, "No, because we'll probably be dismantling it before the paint dries. You know how your sister goes through pets."

It's true. Kelly will act all crazy in love with a pet, but before you know it, she's bored with it, and I'm the one taking care of it. First it was Lola the parakeet, then the turtles Scooby and Dooby, then Pixie the teddy bear hamster. Pixie lasted the longest, about four months, because that's how long it took Kelly to dress poor little Pixie in every doll outfit she owned.

As I was putting the tools away, Freddie rode up on his bike.

"Hey," he said.

"Hey, who?" I asked.

"Hey, you," he replied.

He asked me what I was doing, so I showed him the cat ramp. He didn't seem too impressed.

"I was wondering if I could use your mom's table saw," he said. "It's for my wallet collection."

Freddie makes wallets out of duct tape. He's made about a million of them. Well, maybe not a million, but it seems like that many. Some are pretty simple, but others are real complicated with flaps and accordion-type folds, and pockets for keys and cell phones and stuff.

"Why do you need a table saw?" I asked.

"I want to cut the heads off a few big nails to use them as hinges and weights for some flaps I designed."

"Okay," I said, "the saw's in the barn."

"I thought it was in the tool shed," he said.

"No, the shed was getting too crowded."

81

"But aren't the cats in the barn?" he asked.

"Yeah, but don't worry. None of them are allowed to use the power tools," I said. "Although the day before yesterday, I did catch Pixie the hamster messing with the belt sander."

"No, forget it," said Freddie, shaking his head. "I can't be around cats."

This was a new one for Freddie. He'd never been afraid of cats before.

"Why not, Freddie, are you allergic or something?"

"No, and I can't tell you why. Can you bring the saw out here?"

"You want me to drag that big heavy thing out here all by myself?"

Just then Kelly poked her head out the window and shouted:

I ignored her.

"Freddie, why don't you just get some headless nails at the hardware store?"

"Mahz well," he sighed. "If you don't want to help me, I guess I'll have to. Can you lend me five dollars?"

"LARKIN!" she yelled again.

"When I'm good and ready!" I yelled back. "But why do you need to borrow five dollars, Freddie? You're rich! You get fifty dollars a week allowance."

"Because I don't have any money on me, and it would be easier for me to go to the hardware store from here," he said, "instead of going all the way home first."

"Oh, all right," I said. "Wait here."

I was mad.

He gets all that money every week for doing nothing, and yet he's always broke. What does he spend it on? Duct tape?

I went up to my room and took a five-dollar bill from my secret stash. Kelly saw me when I passed by her bedroom door and followed me down the stairs and out the door.

"Hi, Freddie," she said. "I see you're still buying your clothes at Good Will."

Freddie didn't say anything.

I handed him the money. He tucked it in his shirt pocket and rode off.

"So now you're paying your friends to get lost?"

"Shut up, Kelly," I said.

83

For the first time, I noticed the basket she was holding.

"What's that?" I asked.

"It's a basket, stupid."

"I mean, what's that *in* the basket?"

"It's a soft warm sweater that I'm going to wrap the kitty in."

"Kelly, that's *my* sweater."

"Oh, Larkin, Larkin, Larkin, it's always all about you and your stuff, isn't it? Maybe it's about time you stopped obsessing over your silly material possessions and started focusing on the things that really matter in life, like love, peace, and understanding."

"I hate you," I said.

"Hate you back!" she sang. "Now, put down the Hater-ade, and let's catch us a kitty cat, shall we?"

She turned and strode towards the barn.

Twenty minutes later I was in the hayloft, using a tuna-flavored kibble to try to coax the cat Kelly had selected off a roof beam.

I looked down at Kelly below me, holding the basket forward in case the cat fell, and for a second or two, I felt like Jimmy Stewart in *Vertigo*, peering down the zigzaggy staircase inside the bell tower.

"What if I fall?" I said.

84

"You I don't care about," she responded.

I managed to grab ahold of the cat's tail, and ever so gently, I pulled her towards me. She panicked and tried to jump into the hayloft, but instead landed on my face.

"Ow! Ow! Ow!" I yelled into the cat's belly.

Somehow I was able to find the ladder and climb down.

Kelly pried the cat off my face as I gasped for air and spit out a load of cat fur.

"Oh, my poor traumatized widdle baby," said Kelly, wrapping the cat in my sweater. "Mommy's gonna take real good care of my widdle kitty-widdy."

She carried the cat out of the barn.

I sat there on the floor for a little longer, then yelled, "You're welcome!"

VIVE LA PRANK!

This morning I saw Dalton standing around in the school parking lot with two members of his posse, Omar and Mack—or as I call them, Squishy and Stinky.

It had taken a while, but I'd finally convinced Dalton not to do the stunt he'd wanted to do (toss me off the roof while attached to a chain of backpacks) and instead do a less dangerous prank in our French class.

"Hey, Barkin' Face," he yelled. "Get over here."

He'd spotted me.

I walked towards them.

"It's all right," he said. "We may be way cool, but this area is designated Loser Friendly."

Squishy and Stinky laughed like they'd never heard that one before.

"Okay, whatta ya got to report?" he asked.

"So far, everybody's signed on, except for Bethany Weaver," I said.

Bethany could be a problem. She sits in a desk up front and she's one of those "Teacher, you forgot to give us homework" types.

"So, what are you gonna do about that?" asked Dalton.

"I'm going to talk to her at lunch today."

"Good boy," he said. "I know you'll get it done." He reached over to put a "friendly" Vulcan death grip on me, but I backed away just in time.

Later, while waiting in the cafeteria for Bethany, I thought about Mr. Asher Bivic, our French teacher.

He's totally weird.

He's supposed to be teaching us French, but half the time we can't understand what he's saying in English. And when we can understand his English, what he's saying doesn't make any sense.

He speaks with a very strange accent. It's not French, or even Canadian. I think he's from one of those countries that went out of business.

His sounds a whole lot like the crocodiles in that "Pearls Before Swine" comic strip.

As for learning French, the class is a total waste of time. Most of us are only in the class because Spanish was full.

"So, what did you want to see me about?" asked Bethany, interrupting my thoughts.

"I wanted to talk to you about the French class prank," I said.

Bethany scooted her chair closer to mine and got right in my face. I mean that literally. She's one of those people who practically gets on top of you to carry on a conversation, and it's not a real enjoyable experience.

For one thing, she has bad breath.

"I heard all about it," she said, "and I think it's mean what you want to do to Mr. Bivic."

Suddenly, I realized what her breath smelled like.

When I was a little kid, I sometimes used to fall asleep while chewing on my bed sheet. Later, when I woke up, the damp sheet would be right in my face, and it smelled bad. Real bad. Well, that's what Bethany Weaver's breath smelled like—sheet spit!

"It's not mean," I said. "Nobody gets hurt. It's just a joke. It'll be funny, unlike that other prank Dalton wanted to pull—"

"Dalton Cooke's involved in this?" she interrupted.

"Yeah, it was practically his idea," I lied.

"I find him fascinating," she said, suddenly looking all dreamy like. "He's got that whole primal thing going on. He's what cavemen must've been like if cavemen had shaved their body hair and worked out at a gym five days a week."

"Yeah, well, I wouldn't know anything about that," I said.

"But Dalton Cooke," she sighed, "would never go out with a girl like me."

"As a matter of fact, Bethany," I said, "Dalton has said some very nice things about you."

Sure, I lied, but it was for the cause.

I went on to tell her that Dalton was interested in her, and I guaranteed that if she went along with the prank, Dalton would take her on a date to a restaurant, and even pay for the meal.

And she fell for it.

MISS SADIE, THE LOVE DOCTOR

I was digging out the last of the roots from a dead boxwood in Miss Sadie's backyard, when she told me to drop everything and come inside right away.

"Wipe your feet," she said as I entered the kitchen.

"What's the matter?" I asked her. "Is something wrong?"

"Yeah, you," she said. "With all that sneezing and coughing you're doing out there, you're obviously coming down with something."

"Nah, it's the wind," I said. "It's blowing the dirt and dust up my nose and into my eyes."

"I made you soup—chicken noodle."

There it was, all laid out on the dining room table with cloth napkins and everything.

"What do you want to drink?" she asked. "Root beer or ginger ale?"

"Root beer, please."

"What have you got against ginger ale?" she asked.

"Nothing," I said. "I'm an equal-opportunity carbonated-beverage drinker. Either one works for me."

"Root beer it is, then."

While I was eating the soup, we were looking at pictures of Miss Sadie's family on the wall.

"What was Mr. Grubnik like?" I asked.

"Who, Morty? Oh, he was a sweetheart of a guy," she said, "a real *mensh*, a class act all the way." She leaned forward, looked around like she was telling me a secret, and said, "You know, when he was younger, he was quite the ladies' man."

I scooped another spoonful of soup into my mouth, being careful not to slurp it because, you know, you can't act like a regular slob with cloth napkins and everything.

"What did the ladies like about him?" I asked.

"What *didn't* they like? For one thing, he could really cut a rug."

I didn't know what that meant.

"He was in the carpet business?" I asked.

"No, that means he could really dance. Girls like a man who knows how to dance. Can you dance, Larkin?"

I thought about it.

"I guess so," I said.

I played around with the last noodle at the bottom of the bowl, then cut it in half with my spoon.

"My problem," I said, "is when I meet a girl, I don't know what to say to her to make her like me."

"Just be yourself, and she'll like you just fine."

"Yeah, but what should I *say* to her?"

"Say something nice about her," said Miss Sadie. "Compliment her on her shoes, her earrings, the bow in her hair, or whatever she happens to be wearing, and she'll go on for the next two hours talking about her adventures in accessorizing. And all you have to do is nod your head, say nothing, and she'll walk away thinking you're the greatest conversationalist in the world."

Except for the bow part, it sounded like good advice.

LIGHTS, CAMERA, ACTION

It was prank day.

As we filed into the classroom, I reminded Mr. Bivic that today was the day Kiernan and I would be filming his class for the documentary we were working on for Mr. Iampieri's filmmaking class.

Never mind that neither Kiernan nor I were in Mr. Iampieri's class (we're both freshmen), or that Kiernan wasn't even sure how to operate my mom's little 3.2-megapixel camera. He was tall, so he'd be filming the action from the back of the room, while I would cover the front with my regular old 6.0-megapixel camera.

The bell rang and everybody settled into their seats.

Bethany Weaver was at her desk in the front and she kept turning around to give Dalton the eye. You know, all flirty like. He either didn't notice her, or pretended he didn't.

Mr. Bivic tapped a plastic ruler on his desk to get everybody to shut up and he said, *"Votre attention, s'il vous plaît! Pipple, pipple, s'il vous plaît!"*

He announced that Kiernan and I would be filming in class today and said: "Joo are assepted to bee haff has joo do ever day. Unlee better. Hah. Hah."

Or something like that.

Then he winked at me.

He handed out yesterday's vocabulary quizzes then asked us to open our lesson book to Chapter 21 to review irregular verbs.

On cue, Erin Miller raised her hand and said, "Mr. Bivic, before we do the irregular verbs, would you please go over the colors one more time? I get confused with, like, blue."

"Blue in French is *bleu*," said Mr. Bivic.

"I know how *bleu* sounds," said Erin, "but could you write it on the board, please? I get mixed up with the spelling and all."

He swung around and wrote *bleu* on the chalkboard.

"How about green?" someone else said.

Mr. Bivic turned and wrote *vert* on the board.

Next came orange, then pink.

I noticed that Mr. Bivic was acting kind of unusual, even for him. He was smiling a lot and acting all peppy, waving his arms around, almost like he was conducting an orchestra or something.

And he kept looking at me and winking.

"Yellow!"

He turned, wrote *jaune* on the board, turned back around, looked at me, and winked.

He repeated it again with aquamarine, then silver, then brown. Then I realized that Mr. Bivic was performing for the camera.

I got another wink with purple.

What Mr. Bivic didn't realize was that we were pranking him. You see, every time he turned around and wrote something on the board, all of us moved our desks forward a couple of inches.

With lavender, he turned and winked at Kiernan.

With gray, I got winked at again.

We had surged so far forward in such a short time, that we were already on the verge of pinning him against the wall, and he didn't even notice.

After he wrote *blanc* on the board, he tried to turn around, but he was blocked in and couldn't. He staggered sideways, collided with Bethany's desk, and they both crashed to the floor.

The room erupted in laughter, and everybody jumped up and high-fived and fist-bumped each other. Mission accomplished.

I turned and looked back at Kiernan, and he gave me a thumbs-up. He'd gotten it all.

Bethany helped Mr. Bivic to his feet saying, "Oh, I'm terribly sorry, Mr. Bivic. I had no idea they were going to do this!"

Mr. Bivic stood up, smoothed out his shirt, took a deep breath, and announced, "Making the fun eez a leetle going a long way!"

Then the place really went wild. People were screaming, pounding their desks, and laughing like maniacs.

Mr. Bivic whacked his ruler so hard against his desk that it broke in half. He threw the pieces on the floor and shouted, "I KNOW PAUL IZMUN! I KNOW PAUL IZMUN!" and stormed out the door and down the hall.

"Hey, Pace Man," yelled Dalton, "who's this Paul Izmun dude?"

"I think he said, 'I'm no policeman!'" I shouted back.

"Oh. That's a good one," said Dalton.

And it was.

THE MONICA SOLIS PROJECT

There's this girl in my French class who seems kind of nice.

Her name is Monica Solis.

Right after we played the prank on Mr. Bivic, she came up to me at my locker and said she thought the prank was really funny, and she couldn't wait to see the video.

But even before I could say "Thanks," Dalton Cooke butted in, put his arm around Monica, and said:

Then he led her away, bragging about himself all the way down the hall.

A couple of days later, I saw Monica again.

By that time, I had prepared exactly what I was going to say to her. A bunch of guys (and girls, too) from school were going to go bowling on Saturday night, and I was going to ask Monica to go with me.

As my date.

"Hi, Monica," I said.

"Hi, Larkin!" She seemed glad to see me.

I decided to lead with Miss Sadie's advice and I said, "Nice earrings."

"Thanks," she said.

Then I actually took a good look at her earrings and saw a big hickey on her neck. Wow.

"Larkin?" she said.

"Oh, uh, yeah," I said. "I was wondering if you'd like to go with me to the bowling party Saturday night."

Then she started talking, but all I kept thinking was, *Who gave her that hickey?*

Victor? Shaun? Pony Boy?

And I didn't hear a word she said, which was: "Sorry, but I'm going with my mom and dad to Overton, because they're putting my grandma in a nursing home."

And I'm thinking: *Tyler? Or was it DALTON?*

Then I looked more closely and realized it wasn't a hickey at all. It was a birthmark. What a relief.

"Larkin?" she said.

So I finally said:

And that's how I ruined my chances with Monica Solis.

HAVE I GOT A DEAL FOR YOU

On Saturday Freddie and I took the bus into the city, because Freddie's cousin Jason was selling a camcorder, and I wanted to check it out.

I'd never met Jason and I didn't know much about him. I did know that he's about thirty and writes the instructions in user manuals for phones and other electronic equipment. So when you're reading stuff like: "Press the STOP button to exit programming," there's a real good possibility that Jason wrote that line.

I was looking forward to meeting Jason, not only because he would be the very first professional writer I've ever met but also because when he introduced Jason to me, Freddie would finally have to say my name.

"Jason, this is my friend Larkin."

I mean, how could he *not* say my name?

We only had to walk a couple of blocks from the bus stop to Jason's building, but it took us longer than it should have because Freddie was wearing his bedroom slippers, and his feet hurt.

The building Jason lives in is big, old, and right next to the river. We pressed Jason's button at the door, and he buzzed us in.

The lobby was dark and creepy. There was a big gray chandelier and a huge marble staircase that curved up and around to the second-floor apartments.

We took the rickety old elevator up to the fourth floor and found Jason's apartment, 412. Freddie knocked, and a voice inside yelled, "Come in!"

We went inside the apartment, which was small and crammed with lots of stuff like ski equipment, snowboards, a mountain bike, video games, and boxes and boxes of electronic equipment. I thought it was a pretty cool place because it didn't look like a grown-up lived there.

"Hey, Freddie," said Jason.

"Hi, Jason," said Freddie.

"How are Uncle Ted and Aunt Sharon?" said Jason.

"Okay," said Freddie.

"So, Freddie," I said. waiting to finally hear him say it. "Aren't you going to introduce me to your cousin?"

"Oh, yeah," said Freddie. "Jason, this is the guy I was telling you about."

"Hi," I said to Jason. "I'm Larkin." Then I turned to Freddie and said it again, only louder, "Larkin!"

Anyway, so Jason showed me the camcorder, said it worked fine, and let me try it out.

It seemed to work okay. It wasn't as good as my dream camcorder, which costs $1,200, but this model retails for $800, and Jason was only asking $450—*sweeeeet!*

I told Jason I'd have to talk to my dad about it and I'd let him know in a few days.

Then Jason said he had someplace to go, and he'd walk out with us.

While waiting for the elevator, I said, "This place is pretty old, huh?"

"Yeah," said Jason, "it was built in 1902 as a lodge for an exclusive men's club. It had a ballroom and a restaurant downstairs. The second floor had offices, and the top floors were set up like a hotel. About fifty years ago, after the building had been abandoned for many years, it was converted into an apartment building."

"It looks haunted," I said.

"That's because it is," said Jason.

"For real?" I said. I looked up and down the hallway to see if there were any ghosts loitering about, but the coast was clear.

We got into the elevator.

"One day," said Jason, "when I was going down the big staircase in the lobby, I saw a guy standing at the bottom of the stairs. He was wearing a little tweed jacket and knickers. You know what knickers are, right?"

"Sure," I lied.

We got out of the elevator and Jason continued.

"He was also smoking a pipe. It was vanilla-scented pipe tobacco; I could tell from the smell. I walked past him, then stopped and said, 'I guess you missed the sign,' and I pointed at the No Smoking sign on the wall. When I turned to see what his reaction would be, he wasn't there. He'd vanished."

"Vanished?"

"Into thin air, as the saying goes."

"No way!" I said.

"I haven't seen him since," said Jason, "but now and then I smell the vanilla smoke, so I know he's still around."

As we went out the front door and onto the sidewalk, Freddie mumbled, "Tell him about the cat."

"Oh yeah," said Jason, "the ghost of a cat visits my apartment almost every night. Freddie's seen it. Tell him, Freddie."

"You did?" I said.

"Yeah." Freddie shrugged. "But not really."

Whatever that means.

On the bus ride home I asked Freddie if the ghost cat was the reason he's afraid of cats all of a sudden.

"I'm not afraid of cats," said Freddie. "I just don't want to be around them. Now that I know they can be ghosts, I figure if you're mean to a cat when it's alive, after it dies it could come back and haunt you."

"So be nice to cats," I said.

"That's just as bad," said Freddie. "If a cat likes you, it might come back and haunt you because it likes you so much it wants to hang out with you."

Freddie had a good point. I wondered if you were allergic to cats, would a ghost cat make you sneeze? That could be a problem.

"I got an idea," I said. "Let's spend the night in Jason's apartment and film the ghost cat!"

"No," said Freddie.

"Come on, Freddie," I said, "we'd be filming an actual ghost, not doing one of those fake reenactments they do on those ghost programs. This could be big. If we got footage of an actual ghost, we could make a gazillion dollars!"

"No," said Freddie. "I will never again spend a night in that apartment."

Case closed.

PANDORA, WE HARDLY KNEW YE

I had been out hiking most of Sunday morning with the Buddies and returned home at noon to find my dad in the kitchen making a sandwich.

"How about some lunch, Larkin?" he said. "Your mom bought French rolls yesterday; we can make subs."

So together we made submarine sandwiches and settled down at the table.

I took a bite out of mine and said, "Dad, there's something I've been meaning to ask you."

"Don't speak with your mouth full," he said.

So I chewed, swallowed, then told him about Freddie's cousin Jason and the camcorder he was selling and what a great deal it was and could I borrow $350 from him to buy it?

"I'll pay you back," I said. "I promise."

He took a real long time to answer, and then he said, "I don't think so, son."

I hate when he calls me *son* like that, especially like now, when he's being all cheap, and I'd rather be someone else's son, like Jack Cooke's son. He gives his son Dalton whatever Dalton wants whenever Dalton wants it. A camcorder would be no big deal to Jack Cooke.

"Why not?" I asked.

And I was immediately sorry I'd asked, because I knew he'd tell me the reason why he wouldn't lend me the money, and I didn't want to hear it again.

And so, of course, my dad started in with the bike story.

Here is the condensed version: Two years ago, my dad bought me a new bike, and a month later I left it unchained at the bike rack at the bus stop. It got stolen. He bought me a second bike, and a month later, I chained it to a parking meter, and some guys came along and lifted the bike over the meter and made off with it. Okay, I know it was a stupid thing to do, but back then I was still a stupid kid.

I'm a much smarter guy now.

A much smarter guy who now rides either my old beat-up bike, or Kelly's old beat-up bike, whichever doesn't have a flat.

So, to continue my dad's lecture, if I want to get another big-ticket item, like a camcorder, I'll have to *earn* the money to pay for it.

Lucky for me, my dad's "Lesson of the Bikes" lecture was interrupted when my mom got home. She spends most Sunday mornings at church where she helps to cook and serve meals to homeless people.

"Can I make you a sandwich, dear?" my dad asked her.

"No, thanks," she said, "I've been handling so much food this morning, I've completely lost my appetite." She then sat down next to me, broke off a piece of my sub, and popped it into her mouth.

"Mom!" I said.

"Shh," she whispered, glancing around. "Do you hear that?"

I listened, and I did hear something. It was a series of thumps that seemed to be getting louder and louder, until it sounded like a herd of buffalo charging down the stairs.

It was Kelly, who burst through the door and bellowed, "I've had it! I can't take it anymore!"

"What's the matter, princess?" said my dad.

Kelly was pacing the floor and heaving, as if she were trying real hard to break into tears.

You know, *pretend* tears.

"My life," she said dramatically, with her eyes closed, "is one heaping bowl of warmed-over despair, seasoned with equal dashes of aggravation and angst!"

"Stop it," I said cheerily, "you're making me hungry."

"Shut up, Larkin," she said.

"Now, Kelly, I'm sure you're being overly dramatic," said my mom.

"Look at me, Mother," she said. "I'm a mess! My hands are shaking and my nerves are shot!"

Actually, she didn't look any worse than usual. In fact, she looked a little better because she didn't have that little speed bump on her head.

"What's your problem this time?" asked my mom.

"It's Pandora! She's up all night, every night, jumping on the dresser, pouncing on the bed, swinging from the curtains!"

"Aww, but she's such a sweet little kitty," said my mom.

"She's the Terror Who Never Sleeps! And she won't use the cat door! She sits there and cries when she wants to go out, and again when she wants to come in: *Meeeeeoowwwww*. I can't stand it! That cat has plucked my last nerve!"

"Maybe she'd behave better if you were nice to her," I said, "instead of yelling at her all the time."

"Shut up, Larkin! It's all your fault anyway!"

"*My* fault?"

"Yes, it's because of you that Pandora and those other barn cats are so neurotic."

That really made me mad.

"I did not make those cats, or any cats, neurotic, and if they *are* neurotic, I had nothing to do with making them neurotic!"

Then I turned to my mom and said, "Mom, what does *neurotic* mean?"

"It means nervous, honey," she said, "or having a mental disorder."

"Why do you always take his side?" wailed Kelly.

"I'm not taking anybody's side, Kelly. I'm explaining to your brother what *neurotic* means."

"Well, you tell him that I want that cat out of my room by sundown today!"

Then she stomped out the door, and thumped, thumped, thumped back up the stairs.

"Well," said my mom, "wasn't that delightful?"

"And that was just the matinee," said my dad. "You know how much better her evening performances are."

LARKIN PACE, COME ON DOWN!

I finally got the footage of the French class prank edited together into a four-minute video. I added a clunky polka that goes real well with Mr. Bivic's spinning around and showing off for the camera. In fact, it looks like he's actually dancing the polka.

I posted the finished video online this morning, and it's already had fifty-six hits.

I can't wait to be out of here and making movies for a living.

The problem is I've got three more years of high school, then four years of college. What a big waste of time school is.

I mean, I already know exactly what I want to do with my life. Just give me the proper equipment and a decent budget, and I'll start right now.

Okay, I'll let you in on a little secret. For the past year or so, I've been working on a way to fast-forward my filmmaking career. It's my Master Plan, and this is how it's going to work.

First, I'll have to get to Hollywood. I'll probably hitchhike out there. It's the cheapest way to do it, and depending on the weather, I should be able to get there in four or five days.

Second, when I do get there, I'll go right to Television City in Hollywood and get in line for *The Price Is Right*. I'll already have the ticket I preordered online.

I'll have a fake ID that says I'm eighteen, and I'll be wearing a fake moustache and a little soul patch to make me look older.

And maybe a tattoo.

When the producers come out to pre-interview everybody in line, I'll act real peppy and tell them that I'm an Accidental Genius type who can recite lines from any movie that they can name, and I'd be willing to do it on the show with Drew Carey.

To get on a show like this, it helps to have a weird kind of talent. The weirder your talent, the better your chances are.

Actually, just having a weird name like Larkin should be enough to get me selected to be a contestant.

Third, after I'm seated in the audience and waiting for the taping to start, I'll check my notes.

You see, for the past year, I've been recording *The Price Is Right* every day and making notes of the prices of the items. I've even memorized most of them.

Then, when the announcer yells out: "Larkin Pace, come on down!" I'll be ready, man.

When they bring out the first item for bids, the beautiful Spa-in-a-Box, I'll say "$1,499," which is the exact price. I'll go up onstage, and because I got the price right on the nose, Drew Carey will give me $500 as an extra bonus, and I'll continue on to play a pricing game.

Because I'll know most of the prices, and I'm smart enough to wear running shoes, and not flip-flops like some of those losers who trip all over themselves while playing The Race Game or Bonkers, I'll probably win a lot of stuff. I'd really like to play Plinko or It's in the Bag and win cash, but I'd be down with winning a new car.

But then, and this is really important, because I will win the most in cash and prizes, I'll be the last person to spin the wheel for the Showcase Showdown. After the other two contestants have spun, I'll step up to the wheel, spin, and it'll land on the $1.00, which is worth $1,000. The place will go wild. People will be whistling and jumping around.

Then, when it's time to take the bonus spin, instead of spinning for the $25,000, I'll make an important announcement.

I'll say, "Thank you, kind people of *The Price Is Right.* Your generosity has touched me in a very special place. It means a lot to me. However, I cannot in good conscience spin the wheel again, for I have won enough good, quality, brand-name stuff already. Therefore, I give up my spot in the Showcase Showdown to the second-place contestant, Aileen, that poor old toothless widow from Kentucky."

Then poor old Aileen will fall to her knees in tears, and the audience will chant: "Larkin! Larkin! Larkin!" and they'll have to cut to a commercial.

During the commercial break Drew Carey will tell me that what I did was a first on *The Price Is Right.* He'll ask me to stick around after the show, because he wants to hang out with a great guy like me.

Later, the two of us will go to a fancy Hollywood restaurant where lots of famous people hang out, and I'll order a shrimp cocktail and the filet mignon, medium rare, and a Caesar salad.

We'll be just sitting there talking about stuff, and Drew Carey will get a phone call from his agent or somebody famous, and he'll excuse himself and take the call out on the patio so he won't disturb the other diners if he has to cuss or something.

While I'm sitting there drinking my shrimp cocktail, Steven Spielberg and Ron Howard will come in and sit at the next table. I'll act real cool, and ignore them, like it's no big deal that two of Hollywood's greatest directors are just inches away from me.

Pretty soon they'll start talking about how worried they both are that they'll never be able to make another blockbuster because all the scripts they've been getting are so bad. "There are no good stories out there," Steven Spielberg will say. "Yeah," Ron Howard will say, "maybe all the good stories have already been made into movies."

Then I'll lean over, introduce myself and say, "Gentlemen, I believe I have the story you're looking for."

Then I'll tell them my idea for a movie about this guy and a beautiful shampoo girl who meet on a plane that's flying to Los Angeles. When they land, their families aren't there to meet them, and so they take a cab to the guy's father's house, but when they get there, the father's dead, and the five-year-old stepbrother is now fifty-five years old. So their plane had flown fifty years into the future!

Brooke will play the part of the shampoo girl, and Drew Carey will play the dead father.

That's all I'm going to tell you, except that creatures from another dimension are trying to take over the world, and they're disguised as cab drivers and schoolteachers.

After they hear my story, Steven Spielberg will offer me a million dollars to write the script. He and Ron Howard will co-direct the movie, which will go on to gross $3 billion. My cut will be about $900 million, which will be enough for me to start my own production company and make movies from all my other great story ideas.

And all of this will happen before my sixteenth birthday.

Anyway, that's my Master Plan.

A CALL FROM FREDDIE

I checked last night to see how many hits my French class prank video had gotten, and it was up to 1,690—and that's after being online for only four days.

My mom yelled from downstairs that Freddie was on the phone, so I went down to see what that was all about, thinking something must be up, because Freddie never calls to just chat. He's not a chatting-on-the-phone type of guy.

Out of curiosity, I asked my mom if Freddie asked for me by name. She wanted to know what I meant.

"Did he say, 'Is Larkin there?'" I asked.

"Uh, I guess so," she said. "No, wait. When I answered, he said, 'Hi, Mrs. Pace. It's Freddie.' So I just assumed he wanted to speak to you."

I picked up the phone and said, "Hello, it's Larkin."

"I know," said Freddie. "Can you come over? We have a situation here." He sounded all serious.

"What kind of situation?" I asked.

"Uh, it's something I'm not supposed to tell you about until you get here."

"What are you talking about?" I was pretty annoyed. "Freddie, we're about to have dinner in, like, two minutes."

"You can eat here," he said.

"What are you having?"

"Hold on." Then I heard him say, "Mom, what are you fixing for dinner?"

There was a lot of whispering and stuff, and Mrs. Schnase got on the phone and said, "Larkin, something's happened. We need your help. It's about Ted. Can you come over right away? And please don't tell anybody why you're coming."

How could I tell anybody why I was coming, if even I didn't know why I was coming?

"Okay," I said, "I'll be there as soon as I can."

I told my mom I was going to Freddie's to work on a project, and I wasn't sure what time I'd be home.

I put on my jacket, zipped my camera into the side pocket, took the bike without the flat tire, and pedaled through the dark, cold night to Freddie's house.

Mrs. Schnase sure sounded upset on the phone. Sometimes she gets all emotional and acts kind of crazy. Like the time she called Mr. Schnase when he was on a job in South America and told him to come home right away because she couldn't figure out how their new remote control worked, and she didn't want to miss the season finale of *Dancing with the Stars*.

I thought about what Mrs. Schnase had said: "It's about Ted." Ted is Mr. Schnase, and something must have happened to him. Maybe he fell down the stairs or had a heart attack. But why were they calling me for help? Maybe they'd heard that I'd taken that class last year at the Red Cross and wanted me to do CPR on him.

I hoped not.

I'd feel weird giving mouth-to-mouth to Freddie's dad. I don't think I could give mouth-to-mouth to any man. Or to any woman that looked like a man. I guess I could probably give mouth-to-mouth to a pretty girl. She wouldn't have to be too pretty, but she'd have to be at least as pretty as the plastic dummy we practiced on at the Red Cross.

It's all very mysterious, but then so is Mr. Schnase.

I know he's pretty old. Once on his birthday, I asked him how old he was, and he said he was closer to a hundred than he was to zero. So that means he has to be somewhere over fifty. I know he travels a lot for business. His job is to track down fake microchips. I know he always takes his golf clubs with him when he travels, so I guess there are a lot of fake microchips on golf courses.

I also know that he was married before. Freddie told me that his ex-wife, Linda, took all his money and ran off to California with an aboveground pool guy.

When I got to their house, Freddie was at the kitchen table working on a duct tape wallet. Mrs. Schnase had just taken a plate of nachos out of the microwave. She told me to have a seat.

I looked around but didn't see Mr. Schnase anywhere on the floor.

"Have a nacho," said Mrs. Schnase, sliding the plate to me. Her nachos aren't the greatest. She squirts aerosol cheese on olives and corn chips and nukes it for twenty seconds. And the olives still have the pits in them.

"Oh, Larkin," she said, "the last five hours have been a nightmare, a living nightmare!"

"Where's Mr. Schnase?" I asked.

"Freddie's father is away on a business trip," she said. "He's in Asia, in one of those horrid little countries where nobody speaks proper English and they have flying cockroaches."

"Flying cockroaches?" I said.

"Yes, and while he was at the airport, waiting to board the plane to come home, two men in uniforms pulled him out of line and arrested him! They said they caught him stealing—no, something like stealing. Freddie, honey, what did they say they arrested Daddy for?"

"Smuggling antiquities," said Freddie.

"That's right," she continued, "smuggling antiquities. He took an ashtray from the hotel, is all he did! Those people are a bunch of crooks, and now they want us to pay a $25,000 fine, or they'll haul him off to prison!"

She pulled a tissue out of her sleeve and started to cry.

I felt sorry for Mrs. Schnase and all, but I still couldn't figure out why she'd called me for help.

And then it hit me.

She wants me to help pay the fine.

"Gee, Mrs. Schnase," I said, "I only have $285.75, and that's money I'm saving to buy a camcorder."

"Oh, no, no, no, Larkin," she said, "that's not why I asked you to come here tonight. We have the $25,000. What we need is for you to help us get the money out of the hole in the basement."

Then she led me down the creaky basement stairs where she explained what she meant.

There's a hole in the basement wall that leads to a crawl space under the master bedroom. Many years ago, Mr. Schnase had buried $30,000 in cash in a metal box in the crawl space. He did it because of something called Y2K, which is when everybody thought the world was going to end when computer clocks switched from the year 1999 to 2000.

Because Freddie was afraid of spiders and small spaces, and especially spiders in small spaces, she wanted me to crawl through the hole in the wall and dig up the box of money.

I thought about it for a little while and offered them a deal. I'd agree to dig up Mr. Schnase's cash box if they'd let me film it when they opened the box, and, more importantly, if Freddie would set it up so that the two of us could spend a night at Jason's place to film the ghost cat.

Mrs. Schnase agreed to let me film the opening of the box, but only if I didn't film their faces or say their names.

Freddie agreed to the night in Jason's apartment, but he wasn't real happy about it, if you know what I mean.

I crawled into the hole with a little shovel and started digging in the spot under the brick marker. Freddie held the flashlight for me. It turned out that I didn't have to worry about running into any spiders in that tiny crawl space, because they had all frozen to death.

It seemed like I had been digging for hours, when I finally heard the shovel strike something metal. It was the box. I dug around it and lifted it out of the ground. We managed to get the box through the hole in the wall, and Freddie carried it up the stairs and placed it on the kitchen table.

Mrs. Schnase wiped it off with a damp rag, while I washed my hands and got my camera ready.

"Okay," I said, "don't do anything until I give the word."

I turned the camera on myself and said, "Hi, Larkin Pace here. I'm presently in the home of this typically anonymous family, and we're about to open a treasure chest that's been buried under their typically anonymous home for a very long time."

I aimed the camera at the box and said, "All right, typically anonymous lady, you may proceed."

Mrs. Schnase undid the latch and tried to open the lid, but it was stuck. She tapped the side of the lid with a knife and pulled the handle until it popped open.

"Ah, yes," I said, quoting from *The Treasure of the Sierra Madre*, "I know what gold does to men's souls."

"It's not gold," said Freddie.

"I know, but I don't know any famous quotes about paper money."

Mrs. Schnase gently lifted out the plastic bag, set it on the table, and unraveled the green twist tie. Inside was a stack of cash bound together by a rubber band.

She picked up the stack and tried to lift the corner of the top bill, a fifty, but it wouldn't budge. It was stuck to the stack. In fact, all of the bills were stuck together like they had become one big cash brick or something. When she tried to peel them apart, the edges crumbled and fell away like ashes.

I stopped filming because Mrs. Schnase had begun to cry again.

"What are we going to do now?" she sobbed. "It breaks my heart to think of him rotting away in some rat-infested foreign prison!" She blew her nose into a tissue. "Oh, Freddie, what are we going to do now?"

She walked slowly down the hall and I could hear her in the bathroom, brushing her teeth and gargling between sobs.

"Maybe they'll put your dad on that show, *Locked Up Abroad*," I said, trying to sound all positive. "And people will see it and start a fan club and hire a rich lawyer to get your dad released."

Freddie shrugged and went back to his wallet collection.

Yeah, I guess not. Grumpy Mr. Schnase isn't exactly the fan-club type.

I put on my jacket and went home.

WHY WEASEL'S LIBRARY LADY HATES ME

I went to the school library to return a book of poetry I'd borrowed for Mr. Bivic's French class. He made us find a poem and translate it from English to French, then read it in front of the class.

What a dumb assignment. Most poems are hard enough to understand in English, and when they're being read in French, nobody knows what's going on.

The only good one was read by Thomas Petti, who translated a dirty English limerick into a dirty French limerick.

I gave the poetry book to Mrs. Creighton, the librarian, and I told her it wasn't overdue, but she checked to make sure anyway. She gave me that look she always gives me, like she thinks I might be up to something.

Il y avait un homme de Nantucket...

She's had it in for me ever since last semester when I found this injured pigeon in the parking lot. It couldn't fly, and I was afraid it was going to be run over by a car or eaten by a cat or something, so I tucked it into my jacket and carried it around to my classes all day.

No problem.

That is, until that afternoon, when I took Pete the Pigeon to the library and let him walk around on one of the tables for a little exercise. All of a sudden, Pete hopped on top of a stack of books and took off flying across the room.

It was a miracle!

It's too bad he landed on Mrs. Creighton's head. His feet got tangled up in her hair and, well, it caused a big scene. She kept trying to shoo him off, and he kept flapping his wings, and by the time he managed to break free, she was left with a totally ruined fifty-dollar hairdo. I know that's what it cost because she kept telling me that's what it cost, not including tip.

As I was leaving the library, I noticed Brooke's backpack on a chair. I knew it was hers from the pink "Diva-licious" sticker on the side flap.

So I went looking for her.

I spotted her in one of the alcoves. She was leaning against the back wall, talking to Dalton Cooke. That's right—*that* Dalton Cooke!

A lot of things were going through my mind. Why was she with him? Did she actually like him? Were they going together? Was he the guy I overheard her talking to on her cell phone that night I called her?

No, this couldn't be happening. He's a big dummy. She's smart, real smart. What could the two of them possibly be talking about?

I crept closer to listen.

They didn't seem to be saying anything. In fact, she looked kind of bored. Then finally, she said to him, "What's your story?"

"Story?" he said. "I don't know no stories."

Seriously, is he dumb, or what?

Then she said, "You aren't too smart, are you? I like that in a man."

"Huh?" said Dalton.

I couldn't stand it anymore. She was feeding him a line from *Body Heat,* so I blurted out the next line. "What else you like? Lazy? Ugly? Horny? I got 'em all!"

"Larkin!" Brooke said, all surprised.

Then, to make a dramatic exit, I swung around real fast but crashed right into a metal cart loaded with books. It went flying across the main hall and plowed into a magazine rack, spilling books and magazines all over the place.

After everything settled down, and Dalton had dragged Brooke out of the library laughing his head off, Mrs. Creighton made me stay and clean up the mess and put every single book back exactly where it had been before.

That gave me a lot of time to think about the whole Brooke/Dalton thing. She couldn't really be serious about him. Could she? I mean, he's a major moron. There's no future for her with him, and sooner or later she's got to realize that.

Then I thought of the obvious reason they could never be together in the long run. If they were to get married, her name would be Brooke Cooke.

And that should be a deal killer right there.

PAYBACK TIME

At lunch today, Freddie told me that his dad came home last night.

I got the whole story, but only because I asked about a million questions. That's because Freddie doesn't volunteer much information, unless you keep bugging him about it.

The day after I dug the metal box out of the hole in the basement, Mrs. Schnase took the stack of stuck-together money to the bank. The bank people called in some guy from the Treasury Department, who examined it, measured it, and said it was the real deal.

The bank gave Mrs. Schnase a check for $30,000. She used $25,000 to get Mr. Schnase out of jail, and the rest she spent on a diamond bracelet and some patio furniture.

I told Freddie that it all happened thanks to me, and I reminded him of his promise to set up a sleepover for the two of us at his cousin Jason's apartment so I could film the dead cat.

I meant the dead cat's ghost.

After all, a deal's a deal.

Before Freddie could answer, we were interrupted by Dalton, the scummy creep and girlfriend thief who was in my face saying, "Hey, Barkin' Face, what's the deal with this Bad Breath-any Weaver girl? She's, like, all over me, because she said you promised I'd go out with her."

"Oh, yeah," I said, suddenly remembering the deal I'd made with Bethany. "You promised to take her out on a date to a restaurant if she participated in the French class prank."

"No way," said Dalton.

"Dalton Cooke, you're avoiding me," said Bethany, who popped up right behind him.

"I don't know nuthin' about no date!" said Dalton.

"Don't give me that, you weasel," said Bethany. "A deal's a deal."

Dalton headed for the exit with Bethany following him close behind.

"And it had better be a nice restaurant," she shouted loud enough for everyone to hear, "not one with plastic chairs and pictures of food on the walls!"

"Bethany's right about that," I said to Freddie. "A deal's a deal."

THE UNINVITED GUESTS

My dad came downstairs all dressed up in a tux. He looked good, kind of like one of those guys who shows you to your table at a fancy restaurant.

He and my mom were going to a big banquet in the city and they were going to spend the night in a hotel. That meant I would be left alone here with The Beast. You know, my sister Kelly.

My mom came downstairs next, and she looked great, like a movie star, only better.

"Wow, you clean up real good, Ma," I joked.

I took out my camera and started taking pictures of my mom and dad like they were going to the prom or something. A geezer prom.

"Now help her on with her jacket," I directed my dad. "Okay, now give her a kiss." He did, but instead of a little smooch on the cheek, they went at it full force on the lips, a regular soul kiss, and it lasted a long time, maybe even longer than the kiss between Cary Grant and Grace Kelly in *To Catch a Thief,* which lasted like a half hour or something.

"Disgusting," said Kelly from the kitchen door. "Aren't you two a little old for that sort of thing?"

"No one is ever too old for a little romance," said my mom after they'd unlocked their lips.

I helped carry their bags out to the car, and the whole time they kept giving me instructions:

"Don't let the dogs in the house."

"Be sure to lock both doors."

"Remember to turn off the stove."

And this one from my dad: "Don't torment your sister."

I won't even comment on that last one.

The first thing Kelly said after they'd driven off was, "I hate it when they get like that." She rolled her eyes.

"What's your problem, Kelly?" I said.

"*They* are my problem," she said. "Have you ever noticed that when they're all lovey-dovey like that, they're impossible to deal with? They become a parental unit."

"What are you talking about?"

"If you ask Mom for something, and she says no, when you go to Dad for help, he'll say no, too. That's because they're in sync and they agree on everything. I hate it when parents cooperate with each other."

"Oh, yeah," I said sarcastically, "like you have such a hard time getting everything you want from Mom and Dad."

"Like what?!" she asked, acting all surprised.

"Like everything," I said, "like those stupid dolls that cost a ton of money and you've never even played with."

"That's because they're not toys, they're collectors' items," she said. "My American Girly Doll collection will be worth a lot of money someday."

"And how about all those clothes you never wear?"

"Shut up, Larkin."

"Like the dragon lady jacket."

"You're just jealous because I like nice things."

"'Oh, please, Daddy, I've got to have it, *please*?'" I was doing my impersonation of Kelly. "'And how much does it cost, princess?'" Now I was doing my dad. "'A hundred dollars? Sure, why not? Anything to make my little princess happy!'

"And you never even wear it," I said.

"That's because it wasn't quality merchandise," she said. "It made me look fat."

"What makes you look fat," I said, "is the chocolate chocolate-chip ice cream you cram into your mouth."

So anyway, we argued like that for hours until she went up to her room and slammed her door, and I sat down in the den to edit a couple of videos.

I have never really finished editing the video of the stuck-together money. Even though Mr. Schnase was released from prison and got home safely, I felt kind of bad seeing Mrs. Schnase so upset and crying and everything. I didn't tell anybody about that night, not even Mom and Dad. The video I worked on instead was of this big guy in a little car who nearly ran me over while I was skateboarding in the mall parking lot.

I always carry my camera with me just in case something like that happens. I figure it's one more way I can fast-forward my career as a film director.

I call it My Other Master Plan.

Like if a guy really did crash into me while I was on my skate-board or bike, I'd film everything: the damage, the injuries, the witnesses, even the guy who ran into me. Then I'd edit it into a professional-looking video, complete with cross-cutting and dissolves and close-ups, and even subtitles. I'd add music, so that every time I cut to the guy who ran me over, Darth Vader–type music would play.

Then, when I sue him on one of those TV court shows, like

People's Court or *Judge Judy*, and the judge says, "Tell me what happened," I'll say, "Your Honor, why don't I just *show* you what happened?" and they'll play my video.

Meanwhile, sitting at home watching all this on TV will be Quentin Tarantino or George Lucas or some other famous movie director, and he'll say, "Hey, this kid is good. I could use somebody with his kind of talent to work with me on my next blockbuster project." And he'll have his people contact my people (who are my mom and dad, I guess), and the rest will be history.

The problem with the near-miss I had yesterday at the mall, is I didn't get any good shots. I didn't really have any scrapes or bruises, and my skateboard didn't look any more banged up than it normally looks. I didn't even get a good shot of the guy who almost ran me over, just one long shot of him making a left turn onto the boulevard and giving me the finger.

After I finished editing, I played a couple of online games with Kyle and Ryan, two guys I know from school. Then I fell asleep at the computer.

At about two A.M. I heard the Buddies barking. Then somebody screamed. It was Kelly. I ran upstairs and tried to open her door, but it was locked.

"Kelly, open up!" I yelled.

I heard her telling somebody in her room, "Stay away from me! Don't touch that! Stop it! Stop it!"

Who could it be, I thought, *and how did they get* in *there?*

Kelly flung open the door, and at first, I wasn't sure what those things were in her bedroom. One of them was in Kelly's bed, and the other one was in her American Girly Doll Collection case. Were they tiny bears, or midgets in fur coats?

Oh, I finally realized, they were raccoons!

The one on the bed raised its front paw as if to say, "Hi."

I burst out laughing.

"What's the matter with you?" shrieked Kelly. "Do something!"

But I couldn't stop laughing.

Finally, I said in a voice like Al Pacino's in *The Godfather, Part II*: "In my *home*, Fredo, where my children play with their toys!"

"This is all your fault, Larkin," she yelled in my ear. "Get rid of them. NOW!" Then she stomped down the hall and locked herself in the bathroom.

I looked around the room for something to poke the raccoons with. They smelled real bad, so I didn't want to touch them. I thought about chasing them with the vacuum cleaner, but I instead picked up one of Kelly's American Girly Dolls. The tag on it read "Amber Beth." I held it out in front of me like a vampire slayer would hold a crucifix, and said, "Be gone with you, creatures of the night!"

They didn't budge.

So I took a step forward and hissed at them. The one on the bed bowed his head, leapt onto the windowsill, then squeezed out the cat door.

"You," I bellowed at the other one, "go also from whence you guys came! Return to the darkness!"

Slowly, so very slowly, the other raccoon followed its smelly friend out through the cat door.

"Amber Beth," I said to the doll, "you're one fearsome little cupcake."

I nailed one of Kelly's three-ring binders over the cat door and told her it was safe to return to her room. But the raccoon odor was so bad, she decided to spend the night in our mom and dad's bedroom.

Before she closed the door, she hit me with this one: "I feel like it's November first," she said, "and I'm that discarded jack-o'-lantern whose heart and guts are splattered all over the boulevard of broken promises."

"And good night to you, too," I said.

IT WOULDN'T KILL YOU TO EAT A LITTLE SOMETHING

I think Miss Sadie is running out of chores for me to do.

When I was at her place last week, she'd finally decided to let me dust her pudgy kid collectables—or as she called them, her *tchotchkes*. But instead of dusting them one by one, I saved a lot of time by putting them all in the bathtub and giving them a hot shower.

A SWAN DIVE FOR THE GOOSE GIRL, YEEE-*HAH!*

They seemed to like it.

Then she decided she liked the way the sunroom looked without all that clutter, so when they dried out, we wrapped each of them in newspaper and placed them in a couple of big boxes in the hallway.

When I was at her house today, the only chore she had for me to do was to coax the drawstrings out of the waistbands of three pairs of extra sweatpants. I tried using a knitting needle, a safety pin, and tweezers, but it wasn't easy.

I was doing that chore in the living room where Miss Sadie and I were watching a DVD of *The African Queen*. When Humphrey Bogart gets out of the river and into the boat, I paused the DVD and said, "Here comes my favorite line."

I pressed the PLAY button and said along with Bogart: "One thing in the world I hate: leeches. Filthy little devils."

"This is an old movie," said Miss Sadie.

"Yeah," I said. "Nineteen fifty-one, directed by John Huston, a truly awesome director."

"So how do you know so much about such old movies?" she asked.

"I've watched a lot of them."

"But how do you know so much about them," she said, "and at such a young age?"

"I don't know. I just do," I said. "Like, when I hear a character say something really funny or interesting, I sort of memorize it without trying to."

"Do you also memorize all the things you're being taught at school?"

"No," I said, "because nothing they teach at school is funny or interesting."

"I've never heard of such a thing," said Miss Sadie.

"My girlfriend Brooke is the same way, except she usually has to watch something a few times before she can remember it," I said. "But she's not my girlfriend anymore."

"Not your girlfriend anymore?" said Miss Sadie. "Ah, kids nowadays. What are you, twelve? Thirteen? And already you have an ex? Go figure!"

Then I told her all about me and Brooke, how we played the rainbow in our third-grade class play, how I thought she was my girlfriend but she didn't think so, and how she's all hot now for Dalton Cooke, a guy I can't stand.

"What's this Dalton fellow got that you haven't got?" asked Miss Sadie.

"I don't know, except he's rich and has big muscles and everything."

"Ach! That's all superficial nonsense," said Miss Sadie. "It's what's inside that counts. If she's a smart cookie, she'll realize that you're the real catch and come back to you."

"Yeah, but what do I do in the meantime?"

"You live your life! Study, work hard, be kind to people, and good things will come your way."

"I don't know," I sighed, "that Dalton Cooke ..."

"Dalton Schmalton," she said, waving her hand in the air like she was shooing a gnat. "Stop worrying about who you aren't, and start worrying about who you are.

"I tell you what," she said, "if you want to make the big muscles, maybe you should put down the sweatpants and pick up the boxes of *tchotchkes* in the hallway and carry then up to the attic. When you're finished with that, there'll be a big piece of apple crumb cake waiting for you in the kitchen."

"Apple crumb cake?" I said.

"That's right, *bubeleh*," she said, "because it wouldn't kill you to eat a little something."

MEOW, MEOW, BOO!

Freddie and I were finally going to spend the night at his cousin Jason's apartment to film the ghost cat.

But first, my mom had to get involved. She's never met Jason, so she wasn't about to let me spend the night there until she first called Freddie's mom, then Jason, and asked him a lot of questions. Then, when she was finally convinced that Jason wasn't a crazed serial killer, she told me I could spend the night at his place.

Add that to my list of Ten Things I Hate about Being 14: My mom has to know every place I'm going and every person who's going to be there, like I'm a six-year-old going to my first sleepover.

Freddie and I rode the bus to Jason's. We each took a sleeping bag and a backpack (not an "overnight bag," which my mom called it), and I packed two cameras and plenty of extra batteries, a pair of clean socks, underwear, and a toothbrush.

During the ride, I asked Freddie what the ghost cat looked like.

"I don't know," he said.

"What do you mean?" I asked. "You said you'd already seen it."

"I was there once when it appeared, but I didn't really see it."

"Well, how do you know it was there?"

"Because Jason and his girlfriend said it was there," said Freddie.

"How did they know?" I asked.

"Because they saw it."

"If they saw it," I said, "then why didn't you?"

"I think because I sort of fell asleep on the couch."

I thought it over, then said, "All right, let's make a deal. We'll both stay awake all night if we have to. We won't sleep until we've filmed the ghost. Deal?"

"Deal," he said.

If I thought the building where Jason lives was creepy looking the day I visited it, it was nothing compared to the way it looked at night. The lobby was real dark, with long black shadows zigzagging across the walls, and the hallways were worse. They had these spooky little lights that made a buzzing sound, and the one way down at the end kept flickering like a miniature lightning storm or something.

Inside Jason's apartment he had plenty of lights on, along with his TV and computer, so it wasn't too bad.

Jason turned out to be a pretty good host. He gave us some left-over pizza and a couple of grape sodas, and for dessert he nuked a bag of popcorn. Pretty decent meal, I'd say.

Jason and I played video games while Freddie sat on the couch and did nothing. Actually, he sat on the couch and sulked. Freddie doesn't play video games. So when I play them, he gets all mad and pouts.

But that's okay, I'm used to it.

At about ten o'clock, Jason said he was going to crash because he had to get up at six A.M. to go mountain biking. He told us that the ghost cat could show up at any time now, and that we should dim the lights and turn off the TV so we could see it better. Then he went to his bed, which is behind a screen in the back of the apartment.

Freddie and I rolled out our sleeping bags on the floor and sat there waiting for the ghost cat to appear. He was holding my mom's camera, and I held mine.

We sat there for, like, a real long time.

"This is boring," said Freddie, finally.

"It's supposed to be boring," I said. "That's why it's called ghost hunting."

I must have been getting pretty sleepy, because that didn't even make sense to me.

"That didn't make any sense," said Freddie.

"It did too," I said, all irritated that he'd noticed. "Maybe if we tried talking for a while, we wouldn't be so bored and sleepy."

"What do you want to talk about?"

"I don't know," I said.

We sat there in silence for a little while longer, then I said, "What did your dad say when he got home after being locked up in that steamy foreign prison with all those pickpockets and murderers and whatnot?"

"He said, 'Where did all this friggin' patio furniture come from?'"

Then Freddie and I did something that we hardly ever do. We talked about stuff, lots of stuff. We even got into some arguments.

I told him something Mr. Bivic told our French class.

He told me about the time his dad took the family to Europe, to visit Octavia, the country.

I told him about the time my dad drove us in a rented RV to the Grand Canyon.

He told me why he always likes to watch the Home Shopping Channel.

I corrected his grammar.

He told me a secret about his sleeping bag.

It was after midnight when Jason came out and said we were making too much noise, and he couldn't sleep. "I'm going to crash at Lisa's pad down the hall," he said. "You can call me on my cell phone if you need me. Freddie knows the number."

Then he left.

"Is Jason some kind of a hippie?" I asked. "I mean, with that 'I'm going to *crash* at Lisa's *pad*' talk, and all?"

"I don't think so," said Freddie. "As far as I know, he doesn't burn incense or wear tie-dyed stuff."

There we sat silently, just the two of us, in the haunted apartment.

"Do you hear that?" I asked.

"What?" said Freddie.

"That music, it's kind of like *The Shining*," I said. "Remember that movie? The creepy twin girls? The elevator full of blood? The band playing in the ballroom? I can hear the band, can't you?"

We listened.

"It doesn't sound like a band in the ballroom," said Freddie. "It sounds more like hip-hop in the next apartment."

"Oh," I said.

After a while, the music stopped. I looked at Freddie, and his chin was resting on his chest. His eyes were closed.

"Freddie." I nudged him. "Wake up. Keep your camera aimed and ready to shoot. Look alive!"

After that I don't remember much, because I fell asleep.

At about two A.M., there was a loud thud, and we both woke up.

"What? What happened?" I said. "What was that?"

"Th-Th-There's s-s-something in here," said Freddie, "and it's b-b-behind the TV."

I heard something moving back there.

Suddenly, a big black shadow sprang across the wall and landed with a thud in the corner.

We craned our necks forward to see what it was. My heart was bumping around in my chest like shoes in a dryer. I switched on my camera and slowly got to my feet. I crept closer, closer, towards the corner. It was dark, so I reached over and clicked on the lamp next to the TV.

I aimed my camera at the corner where it had gone and began filming. I looked at the monitor. There was nothing there.

I glanced over at Freddie. He'd pulled his shirt over his head. "Freddie," I said, "there's nothing in that corner!"

"It jumped there and then it vanished!" he said.

"It was the ghost!" I yelled. "Get up!"

Freddie jumped up and ran around behind the couch, and I was right behind him.

"It's real! We saw it! What do we do? What do we do?" We were yelling at each other.

"Call Jason," I said.

"You have to call him," said Freddie. "I don't have a cell phone."

"Oh, right," I said, "I forgot." I leaned over the couch and took my cell phone out of my backpack. "What's his number?" I asked.

He said the number slowly, and I carefully punched each of the keys. We were both breathing hard. My hands were real cold, and so was the back of my neck. The whole room seemed to have chilled. I pressed the last number, a nine, and held the phone up so we could both hear Jason answer.

Suddenly, a shrill sound pierced the silence. We both dove over the couch and tumbled onto the floor.

The sound was music. It was a song. It was "La Cucaracha," and it was coming from Jason's cell phone on the kitchen counter.

"Now what?" I said.

"Hmmm, maybe we should answer it," said Freddie.

"Are you crazy?" I hollered at him. "IT'S *US* CALLING!"

I ran for the door, opened it, and poked my head into the hallway. Freddie was at my back. The hall looked even scarier than it had earlier that evening, and that one flickering lightbulb didn't help matters much.

We closed the door and decided we'd be better off inside the apartment, as long as we didn't go anywhere near the TV, the corner next to the TV, or near anything the ghost cat may have touched.

We decided to lock ourselves in the bathroom and remain there until Jason returned in the morning.

And that's exactly what we did. We didn't waste our time in there, though. We took the cameras and filmed each other talking about the experience, sort of like *The Blair Witch Project* or *Paranormal Activity*, but on a much smaller budget.

And in a bathroom that wasn't the cleanest bathroom in the world, if you know what I mean.

THE ANY GIRL AT ALL PROJECT

I was all set for the freshman dance.

Lifting heavy boxes of collectables and eating Miss Sadie's apple crumb cake didn't do a whole lot to build up my muscles. So I came up with another way to make myself look big.

146

I read someplace that in order to make themselves look a lot bigger on camera, a lot of young Hollywood actors used to wear lots of T-shirts under their regular shirt. And I figured if it worked for Warren Beatty, maybe it'll work for me.

There was a good chance that Brooke would be at the dance with Dalton, but I had a feeling that once she saw me looking all big and buff and dancing with a bunch of other girls, she'd get totally jealous and be all sorry I wasn't her boyfriend.

I paid for my ticket at the door, and Mrs. Pugh gave me a sheet of paper with rules. There was to be no freak dancing, dirty dancing, or grinding. Boys were to leave their shirts on at all times, and the outside doors would be locked at 8:30 and remain locked until 11:00.

"Excuse me," I said to Mrs. Pugh, "but why are the doors going to be locked?"

"That's so no older kids or non-students can crash the party and cause trouble."

I looked into the auditorium and saw Dalton Cooke by the refreshments table.

"Mrs. Pugh," I said, "speaking of older kids and troublemakers, did you know that Dalton Cooke is in there? He's way old, almost seventeen, and I thought only freshmen were allowed at the freshman dance."

"Oh, dear," she said, and she leaned over and said something to

147

the lady seated next to her. They kept their voices real low and talked back and forth for a while. Then Mrs. Pugh said to me, "Well, it seems that regardless of his age, Dalton Cooke is registered as a freshman."

"Oh, right," I said, "I forgot that he's making a career out of being a high-school freshman."

I entered the auditorium and mingled around a bit. I said hey to a few guys I know, and Bethany Weaver came up to me and said, all squinty, "Larkin, you look different."

"Yeah," I said, "I've been working out a little."

I saw Brooke with a group of girls. I caught her eye and nodded, then walked away, too cool to linger.

Mrs. Pugh got onstage with a microphone and welcomed us to the dance, reminded us of the rules, and made some other announcements that nobody listened to. Then she left and the music started.

I went over to a girl I didn't know, but who looked kind of familiar, and asked her to dance. She said okay, and we went at it. She swayed side to side acting all bored like girls do when they're dancing. I was finding it difficult to move my arms and upper body very much, so I just jumped around until I got tired.

Three songs and three girls later, I was hot, sweaty, and my legs hurt.

My next dance was with a real good-looking girl named Nina. She was taller than me, but I didn't care. I spotted Brooke with Dalton, so I pulled Nina over to where they were dancing. I wanted to make sure that Brooke got a good look at me with Nina.

When we were right alongside Brooke, I said to Nina, "You're a good dancer." Nina nodded, looking like she wanted to be someplace else.

"A revolution without dancing," I said to Nina, "is a revolution not worth having."

"What?" said Nina. "I can't hear you over the music."

I repeated the line, this time shouting as loudly as I could, "A revolution without dancing is a revolution not worth having!"

"What are you talking about?" said Nina, who sounded very annoyed.

"It's from *V for Vendetta!*" I yelled.

"What?!" yelled Nina.

I put my fingers in my ears to block out the music, and yelled at full force, "The movie, *V FOR VENDETTA . . .*"

It's too bad I hadn't noticed that the music had ended abruptly, because if I had, I would have been aware that the only sound echoing through that huge auditorium at that moment was the sound of me shrieking at the top of my lungs, "VENDETTA! VENDETTA! VENDETTA!"

When I did realize what had happened, I could feel my face getting red. Everyone was looking at me. Nina took a few steps back, then turned and walked away, shaking her head as if to say, "Nuh-uh, I'm not with this fool."

Then everyone started to laugh: Brooke, Dalton, Bethany, every girl I'd danced with, everyone. It occurred to me that the entire freshman class was laughing at me.

I forced a fake smile and headed over to the refreshments table. Sweat was pouring out of every part of my body. The DJ cranked up the next song, a slow number, and couples went back to dancing again.

I found a chair and downed three bottles of water. I was hot, so hot, but not in a good way, so I decided to take off some of those shirts.

I staggered down the hall to the men's room. As soon as I opened the door, the first guy who saw me said, "Hey, Vendetta!" Soon every guy in the place was chanting, "Vendetta! Vendetta! Vendetta!" with their fists raised. It was like some kind of a lavatory lynch mob.

I went back into the corridor and tried to open the door to the quad, but of course, it was locked. I needed someplace cool where I could lie down.

I finally found it under the staircase and stayed there until long after the dance had ended.

IT'S "TAKE YOUR KID TO WORK ON YOUR DAY OFF" DAY

I was glad it was spring break. I needed time away from school and all the people who'd been at the freshman dance and would right now be reminding me of it.

I was hoping that a whole week would give everybody enough time to forget about it and move on to the next stupid thing done, I hoped, by somebody else.

I was just happy that nobody at the dance had filmed my performance and posted it on the Web. Or if they did, they hadn't posted it yet.

The other good thing is that most of my friends are not the type of guys who dance anyway. It's not that they're losers; they're just not dance-y types. And from now on, neither am I.

My dad asked me if I wanted to take a ride with him over to the college, and I said sure. It had been raining for the past three days, and I was looking to get out of the house.

On the way, we talked about movies we'd seen recently, and about the Oscars and who should have and shouldn't have won.

He asked me what was going on with me at school, and I said, "Nothing." I didn't tell him about the freshman dance, but I did tell him about this notebook blog I'm writing. He said he'd like to read it sometime, and I said, "No way, I'll probably never be able to show it to my family, or anybody I've written about, including myself." I told him I was going to put it in a time capsule and not let it be opened for a hundred years.

At the college, there were only two other cars in the parking lot, and the building was, like, totally deserted. When we walked to his office, our footsteps echoed down the corridor. "This would make a great location for a slasher movie," I said. "You could have a big mutant-type guy with yellow eyes and nasty-looking teeth like he'd eaten too many blueberry tarts, carrying a bloody sword and stalking a beautiful cheerleader."

"Sounds a bit clichéd, don't you think?" he said.

"Okay," I said, "instead of a cheerleader, we'll make it a shampoo girl."

"A what?" my dad asked.

But before I could answer, a door swung open, scaring us both so hard that we squealed like little girls.

It was Doug Cleary, another English professor at the college and a friend of my dad's. "Hey, Marty, Larkin, what are you guys doing here?" he asked.

It was kind funny hearing him call my dad "Marty." Only my grandmother and my aunts call him that.

My dad explained that we were here to pick up a few things that were stored in his office.

"And, Larkin, look at you," said Doug Cleary. "You've really grown since the last time I saw you."

"Yeah, I wish," I said.

The three of us walked together to my dad's office, and the two of them talked a lot about people I didn't know and about things they'd done together. Doug made my dad sound like a fun guy.

From the closet in his office, my dad took out a big box of movies and an old eight-millimeter movie projector that we were going to take home with us.

Just before we were about to leave, Doug asked me if my dad acted as crazy around the house as he does at school. Like, does he do his impression of Shakespeare's Romeo as performed by Rocky Balboa?

"No," I said. I didn't know what he was talking about.

"Aw, Marty," said Doug, "you're holding back from your very own son? Do it! Do it!"

"Yeah, come on, Dad," I said, still kind of confused, "please?"

So he did it, and he sounded just like Sylvester Stallone in *Rocky:*

He did this whole long speech, and I've got to admit, it was pretty funny.

So, there. I'm writing something nice about my dad. Maybe I will show him this notebook blog sooner than one hundred years from now.

Let's make it ninety-nine years from now.

WHEN A BUDDY NEEDS A BUDDY

I was in my room working on a project for art class. We had to make a collage, and the theme of it was supposed to be "blue."

So I was searching the Internet for blue images, and Photoshopping them together to form an upside-down smiley face, which I guess you could call a frowny face. I chose a frowny face because blue is not only a color, but it means sad, too. So then my collage would be, like, blue *squared*.

But I finally decided to do it as a smiley face after all, because that would make the collage ironic. You know: blue, but happy!

That would surely get me an A because teachers love irony. It makes them feel all warm inside. Or, maybe because it's ironic, they expect to feel warm inside but actually feel kind of chilly instead.

My phone rang, and the caller ID said it was Brooke.

Since the freshman dance, I'd only seen Brooke a couple of times at school, but we hadn't said much of anything to each other. I'd texted her at least twice, but she hadn't responded.

"Hello?" I answered, like I thought maybe it was some kind of trick.

"Hi, Larkin," she said. It was Brooke.

"Hey," I said. "I texted you a few times, but—"

"I know," she interrupted, "but I've been so busy lately that I didn't get a chance to get back to you."

"That's cool," I said, trying to sound cool.

"The reason I'm calling," she said, "is to ask you a favor. As you probably know, ever since Misty died, things haven't been the same around here."

Misty was her little dog that died last year.

"Oh, yeah, that was sad," I said.

"Thank you," she said. "Well, my mom and I have been talking it over, and we've decided that it's about time we got another dog, and we were wondering if we could come over and adopt one of the Buddies."

"Uh, yeah, sure," I said.

I sounded real calm when I said it, but inside I was jumping up and down and yelling. I knew that once she was here and spent some time alone with me, I would activate my killer charm, and she'd be all powerless to resist and she'd fall madly in love with me all over again, and we'd live happily ever after.

Or at least through the summer.

"How soon can you get here?" I asked.

"We were thinking of doing it the Saturday after next."

"The Saturday after next?"

"Yes," she said, "we want to wait until my dad is out of town."

"Oh, okay," I said, "I'll see you the Saturday after next."

I hung up the phone and did a little dance of joy. Actually, it was more like a big monkey madness jungle stomp fest.

It lasted until I saw Kelly standing at my door.

"You are such a pathetic mess," she said.

"Yeah," I said, "but now I'm being a pathetic mess in the privacy of my own room!"

And I slammed the door in her face.

THE BIG SECRET

When my mom picked me up from Miss Sadie's this afternoon, instead of going right home, she drove into town to pick up a check for a job she'd done last week. The sun had just about set when we got there, and she found a parking spot almost right in front of Yuddy's Curl Up & Dye Hair Salon. She told me to wait in the truck and left the keys in the ignition so I could listen to the radio.

So I was flipping through the channels, trying to find something to listen to other than commercials for discount car insurance, credit dentistry, and Macaroni Grill, and I noticed this short, four-legged thing walking along the sidewalk.

At first I thought it was a possum, but once it moved into the circle of streetlamp light, I saw that it was a dog. It looked like it might be a Chihuahua or a miniature terrier of some sort.

There was nobody with it, and it wasn't wearing a collar.

It sniffed at Yuddy's front door, and headed towards the truck. I turned down the radio so it wouldn't suspect that I was spying on it or anything.

I figured it might be either lost or abandoned, and maybe I should take it back to the farm, and come back later to post signs in the neighborhood saying I'd found it.

I got out of the truck and walked very casually towards it. It stopped as soon as it saw me. I crouched down very slowly and held out my hand as if I were holding a treat. "Come here, buddy," I said.

The dog turned and ran back towards the hair salon, where it made a sharp right turn, scooting under a wooden gate that was between Yuddy's and the shop next to hers. I opened the gate and peered down the long narrow passageway that led to the rear of the buildings. It was completely dark, except for a patch of dim light at the end, where the little dog had stopped. It seemed to be waiting to see if I would follow it.

I did.

I made my way through the dark passageway very cautiously, in case I ran into something hidden in the darkness, like a trash can or a bicycle or a crouching vampire.

I made it to the end, where I found a small area, almost like a courtyard. There were some trash cans there, a stack of wooden boxes, and a couple of tires, but no dog.

There was a second dark passageway, which led farther back, so I followed it. I wound up next to a big Dumpster in an alley.

There was no sign of the dog.

I tried calling him again, saying, "Here, buddy. Come here, boy." But no luck.

Then I heard voices.

Three guys were in the alley walking towards me. I didn't want them to see me, so I ducked into the passageway and pressed my back flat against the wall.

Their voices sounded angry, and I could tell by some of the words they were using that there was a pretty good chance they weren't returning from a Bible study class.

I kept very, very still, but there was a problem.

I felt a sneeze coming on, and it was going to be a big one.

I knew if I tried to hold it in, I could pop an eardrum, so I did the next best thing. I pressed my jacket hard into my face and let the sneeze explode out of my mouth and nose. Sure, my jacket was covered in snot and spit, but the heavy fabric had absorbed most of the sound. I hoped.

"Did you hear that?" one of the guys said. He stopped and looked in my direction.

I held my breath and didn't move.

"Ain't nuthin,' man," said one of the other guys, "probably a rat or somethin'."

They continued on their way, and I heard one of them say, "We oughta kill it."

"You crazy, man?" said the other one. "Do I look like a sterminator to you?"

When they were finally out of sight, I hurried back through the passageway and into the little courtyard. There was some light coming from an upstairs window. I looked up and saw the little dog I had been chasing. He was perched on the back of a chair and looking at me as if to say, "Will you get lost, please, so I can resume my evening stroll?"

Then I saw the little doggy door he must be using to make his escapes.

The other source of light was coming from a small window in a very large metal door. I decided to take a peek inside, but the window was kind of high up, so I had to stand on a wooden box.

I was looking into Yuddy's hair salon from the back door. Up near the front counter I saw my mom talking to Yuddy. I recognized Yuddy because I'd been here lots of times with my mom. Her real name is Yudmilla, but she shortened it to Yuddy when she came here from Russia. Every time I see Yuddy, her hair is a different color. Right now it's blonde. She looks kind of like that lady on *60 Minutes*, only worse.

160

I looked around, hoping to spot a shampoo girl or two, but no luck. I've been working on an idea for a movie that'll be one of my first feature films. It's sort of like *Charlie's Angels*, but not as dumb, and instead of being about a team of beautiful private detectives, it'll be about a team of beautiful shampoo girls.

I didn't see any shampoo girls, but I did see a guy sitting in a salon chair. I could tell it was a guy because he was pretty big. There was aluminum foil on his head and pieces of his hair were poking through the foil.

It looked like he was wearing one of the costumes I'd put together when I made my first science-fiction movie: *It Came from A Million Miles That Way!* I think I was about nine when I did it.

As I was comparing the aluminum foil on his head to the aluminum foil helmet I'd made for my movie, he spun around in his chair, and I saw his face in the mirror.

I could hardly believe what I saw.

It was Dalton Cooke!

I nearly fell off my box. I looked again, and sure enough, it was Dalton. What was he doing here, and what was that stuff on his head? Maybe he was involved in some kind of weird scientific experiment, like trying to keep out mind-control waves or something.

Suddenly, it occurred to me that I'd left my mom's truck with the keys in it and the radio on. She would probably die from a heart attack if her truck wasn't there, or even worse, if it was there with the keys in it, the radio on, and me on a box in back of Yuddy's spying through the window!

I ran back to the truck, thinking I could always blame it on that dumb dog.

I jumped into the front seat just seconds before my mom came out of Yuddy's.

"You're certainly out of breath," she said, snapping on her seat belt. "What's wrong?"

"Oh, nothing," I said. "I was just singing along to a song on the radio."

"Oh," she said, and she started the ignition. "What happened to your jacket?" she asked.

I looked down at all the snot and spit. "Oh, uh, it was a very *sad* song," I said, "and I guess I got a little carried away."

Am I quick, or what?

On the ride home, I asked my mom about the tinfoil-hair thing. She explained that it's a process that a woman goes through when she's having highlights added to her hair. "Tips and highlights," she called it. "It's a fancy, and expensive, way of having your hair dyed."

Did you notice that she referred to the person as a *woman*?

So big strong tough guy Dalton Cooke is having his hair dyed— just like a *woman*.

Wow, this is major.

THE SATURDAY AFTER NEXT

From my bedroom window I saw Brooke and her mother drive up.

I checked myself in the mirror. Brooke always used to like it when my hair was kind of messed up, so I went to the bathroom, splashed water on it, and massaged it around a little. I tried to make it stick up—you know, to make me look taller.

I went downstairs.

They were in the living room, where Brooke's mom was making a big deal about some cabinets my mom had built.

"You did all of this yourself?" said Brooke's mom. "I've been looking for something exactly like this for my office!"

"Gee, Pam," said my mom, "I'd be more than happy to work with you on something like this. If you have the time, I have plenty of catalogs we can look through for ideas."

"But, Mom," said Brooke, who was standing at the front door, "what about the dog?"

"I think you and Larkin can probably handle that," said her mom. "Why don't you go take a look at what's available, narrow it down to a couple, and I'll be out later to help you decide."

"Yeah, Brooke," I said, "we can audition the Buddies."

"Just remember, Brooke," added her mom, "we don't want a big one or a slobberer. The last thing we need is a big, drooling dog slobbering all over our furniture and new carpets."

So Brooke and I went outside, and I opened the gate of the dog run and let them all out. They raced around the barn, as they usually do, and Brooke and I tossed tennis balls to them, flung Frisbees, and played hide-and-seek until they tired us out.

"Is that the end of the audition?" asked Brooke.

"No, that's just the beginning," I said. "Now I'm going to play the guitar, and you're going to sing to them."

"I don't get it," she said, "that sounds like *we're* auditioning for *them*."

"No," I explained, "we'll be auditioning the audience. They'll be the audience, and whichever one can tolerate our singing the longest wins the audition."

The Buddies followed us around to the back of the barn to a little platform where Brooke and I sang two songs. The Buddies only stuck around for one number, then they took off after a squirrel.

It felt great being with Brooke again. She was laughing and acting crazy just like we used to whenever we got together.

We even did a short scene from *Batman Returns,* where she played Catwoman and I played Batman.

"You're catnip to a girl like me," she purred, "handsome, dazed, and to die for."

"Mistletoe can be deadly if you eat it," I said.

"But a kiss can be even deadlier if you mean it," she said. "You're the second man who killed me this week, but I've got seven lives left."

"I tried to save you," I said. I pulled her towards me and I kissed her right on the lips, slowly, like I really meant it, with my eyes closed and everything.

"Oh, Larkin," she said.

"Hey, that's not your line," I said.

"I don't think of you that way," she said.

"Oh, but Dalton Cooke—*him* you think of that way!" I was mad.

"Dalton's a very nice person," she said. "He might not seem like it all the time, but that's because he has issues, big issues. You don't know him the way I do."

"Oh, yeah? Well, he dyes his hair!" I blurted out.

"What?"

"I saw him with my own eyes in a hair salon."

"Really?" she said, "at a salon? I'm surprised. I always thought he did it himself. It's not a real professional-looking job, whoever's doing it."

"You knew about this?" I was kind of shocked.

"Yeah, of course," she said. "What's the big deal?"

"The deal is, he's a *guy* who dyes his hair," I said.

"So, lots of guys do it," she said. "My cousin Anthony has been dyeing his hair since he was twelve years old."

"Is he the cousin who eats paper?"

"He doesn't do that anymore," she said, "not since he's being seeing a therapist."

And, well, that's pretty much how things ended between me and

Brooke. Our moms came outside looking for us, and Brooke told them she'd decided on a dog. She chose the one I thought she was going to choose: a white poodle/terrier mix that looked a lot like her other dog, Misty.

She decided to name her Stella.

But she'll always be Buddy to me.

MY BIG BREAK

Something happened today that's so weird, I'm not sure that it really did happen.

Dalton came up to me after school this afternoon and told me that the French class prank that we'd pulled was kind of lame, and he had an idea for another bigger and better prank.

It involved releasing some guy's boa constrictor, or maybe a live deer (or maybe both), in the cafeteria or in the auditorium during assembly, and he wanted me to film it.

Instead of just saying no and walking away, I stuck around and argued with him about it until I missed the school bus.

He said, no problem, because a guy he knew was picking him up to go work out at some gym someplace, and they could drop me off at whatever bus stop worked for me. And that way, the two of us could spend more time in the car discussing his dumb prank.

So Dalton and I got into the backseat of this old clunker that

Dalton's friend Ivan was driving. Also in the front seat was a guy named Sam, who was talking on a cell phone.

Both of them seemed to be a whole lot older than me and Dalton. Ivan had tattoos all over his arms, and one on his neck that looked like a rotten banana, but I found out later it's supposed to be a samurai sword.

Meanwhile, Sam was yelling at somebody on the phone and acting all mad. Then he slammed it down on the seat and said, "Those stupid kids have screwed up everything!"

It turns out that Sam is a director of TV commercials and he was about to begin work on one, but two of his teenage actors bailed on him to go to a skate competition in Ohio. So now he needed two young actors to be in a commercial he was shooting for a donut place.

"How about these two?" said Ivan, meaning me and Dalton.

Sam twisted around and looked at us. "Do either of you dudes know how to use a skateboard?" he asked.

"Well, yeah," I said, rolling up my pant leg to show him the scar on my knee that I got when I hit a crack in the pavement and skidded facedown thirty feet across the parking lot of Downy Woods Middle School.

He explained that the commercial was for Farkus Family Donuts, that he could only pay us $100 each, that we'd need written approval from a parent or legal guardian, and that the shoot was nine o'clock Saturday morning at a place downtown.

I got Sam's business card and wrote down a whole bunch of other stuff he told us.

After they dropped me off at the bus stop, I walked the rest of the way home, and I kept thinking that this was some kind of a dream. Yesterday I was just a nobody, and two days from now, I could maybe be starring in a TV commercial.

I imagined myself going from this commercial to more commercials, then a TV show, then feature films. Once I became a big movie star, I'll have it written into my contract that I get to direct the movies they want me to star in, and even produce them. By the time I'm nineteen, I could be the most powerful person in all of show business!

Awesome.

When I got home and told my dad about the donut commercial, he didn't seem all that impressed. He said he'd have to speak to this Sam guy, so I gave him all the information, and he went into the other room to call Sam.

Kelly just sat there and didn't say a word. I could tell she was jealous that I was going to be a big TV star.

"Maybe I could ask the director if there's a part in the commercial for you," I told her. "I imagine there are trolls who eat donuts."

When my mom, who was just getting home from work, walked in the room, Kelly jumped up and said, "Mom, Larkin was hitchhiking today and got a ride with a deranged maniac who wants to put him in a sleazy movie!"

"Oh, Larkin," my mom said, sounding all disappointed, "you were hitchhiking?"

"No," I said, but before I could explain what really happened, my dad came in and said, "It seems to be on the level. I spoke to the director and checked out his Web site, and although he's strictly local and low-budget, his work does have some merit."

Then my dad said some of the greatest words I've ever heard. "Larkin," he said, "I'll accompany you to the shoot on Saturday."

"That is so typical of the way things work around here," said Kelly. "Larkin always gets whatever Larkin wants, and it's not fair! What about me? What about *my* needs?"

"What needs are you talking about?" asked my mom.

"Well, after going through this entire ordeal," she said, "at the very least, I think I deserve a new leather jacket."

And the sad thing is, she meant it.

SHOOT!

I made my dad get to the studio where they were shooting the donut commercial an hour early, just to make sure we weren't late.

Nobody was in the studio except a guy with a ponytail who told us the crew was shooting another segment of the commercial about two blocks away and they'd be here shortly.

"That means they're on location," I told my dad.

Soon Dalton and his dad, Jack Cooke, arrived, followed by Sam the Director, his crew, and an old man with a cane. Everybody introduced themselves, and a girl with a clipboard gave my dad and Dalton's dad a bunch of papers to sign.

Director Sam showed me and Dalton the set and explained that the scene was supposed to be taking place at a skate park. We would be performing in front of a green screen, but on TV it would look like there were skaters zipping around behind us.

I had about a million questions, like where were our scripts, and what about wardrobe, makeup, and hair, and did he want me to get my own personal skateboard out of the car?

He said that there was no budget for hair or makeup, he would be providing the wardrobe and props, and because we only had one line, there was no need for a script.

He described the scene for us. Dalton would be sitting on a park bench, about to unwrap a granola bar, but he has second thoughts and says, "Why would I want a dried-up old granola bar?" He tosses it over his shoulder, and I catch it as I ride by on my skateboard, and Dalton continues: " . . . when I can have a delicious

Farkus Family Donut?" Dalton next takes a big bite out of a donut he pulls from the bag on his lap, and he goes, "Mmmm . . ."

"When do I say my line?" I asked Director Sam.

"You don't have a line," he said. "You just skate by, catch the granola bar, and skate off."

This was kind of disappointing and not how I thought it would be. How was I going to be discovered if I didn't have any lines?

"Denise!" Sam yelled. "Get the board, the helmet, and the shorts for . . . ?" He looked at me like he'd forgotten my name.

"Larkin," I said.

"For Larky here," he said.

Larky?!

A crabby-looking woman handed me a helmet and shorts and said, "Put these on."

"Where's the dressing room?" I asked.

"Dressing room?" she said. "Get real. You can go put them on behind that crate."

I ducked behind the crate, pulled off my pants, and put on the shorts and helmet. I returned to Sam and said, "Excuse me, but aren't these shorts kind of big?"

He looked at them and yelled, "Denise, what's with these shorts? I've seen smaller circus tents."

"Well, when you told me to get a small," she yelled back, "I didn't know you meant a *boy's* small! How was I supposed to know he was so tiny?" She looked at me like it's *my* fault I'm short.

Thanks a lot, Denise, I thought. *Yours is one more name I can add to my Least Favorite People List. I'll move you right up to the top, above Dalton and Kelly.*

Director Sam had us do two run-throughs—you know, rehearsals—and everything went fine.

Then we started rolling, and on the first take I sort of missed catching the granola bar because Dalton threw it too hard. On the second, third, and fourth takes, Dalton messed up his line.

I could see his dad pacing back and forth behind the camera.

On the fifth take, as I skated out, my shorts fell down, tripping me up. What made it even worse was I was wearing my X-Men underpants, and everybody saw them. Well, hey, when I put them on that morning, how was I supposed to know they were going to wind up on TV?

On the next take, Dalton threw the granola bar so hard it ricocheted off my helmet and smacked him on the back of the head.

On the one after that, we got it right until the very end, when Dalton reached into the bag and came up empty-handed. He'd eaten all of the donuts.

During the break, when they were refilling the bag, Dalton's dad got right in Dalton's face and talked to him like a boxing manager talks to his fighter, but instead of saying stuff like: "Come on, you can do this! I know you got it in you! Get in there and prove it!" his dad was telling him he was an idiot and a loser and using some pretty serious cuss words.

Then Sam pulled Dalton's dad aside and told him to "take it easy, man."

I was feeling kind of bad for Dalton and went over and told him there was a bottle of water under the bench if he was thirsty. He reached under, saw the bucket, and said, "What's this for?"

"That's where you're supposed to spit out the donuts," I said. "Didn't you read the instructions? You weren't supposed to eat anything before you came here this morning, and you're not supposed to swallow the donuts."

Dalton said something I'm not allowed to repeat, and we did the next take.

Dalton blew his line again, but this time his father went ballistic, yelling and cussing at Dalton in front of everybody. Sam told Dalton's dad to put a lid on it, and the old man with the cane (who I found out later was Theo Farkus, the president of Farkus

Family Donuts), started swinging his cane around and knocked over a lamp.

Then everybody started yelling, except my dad, who calmly walked up and put his arm on Mr. Cooke's shoulder. Dalton's dad turned and took a swing at my dad, who quickly blocked the punch with his arm like he was a ninja warrior or something.

It was awesome.

My dad led Dalton's father over to the corner, where they talked quietly for a while. Then my dad said they were going to take a little walk, and the two of them left.

Things settled down and we did another take. It all went perfectly until the very end, when Dalton shoved the donut into his mouth. He stopped. His face turned kind of green, and about a dozen Farkus Family Donuts erupted from his stomach out his mouth and into the bucket under the bench.

"Okay, that's a wrap," said Sam.

"But we didn't get one right," I said.

"There were a couple of halfway decent takes that I can edit together to make one that will work," he said.

A girl dressed as a ballerina and an older lady were standing by, ready to film the next segment of the commercial.

I put on my pants and went outside. Dalton was in the car with his dad, who pealed out like he was in *Gone in Sixty Seconds* and roared down the street.

On the ride home my dad and I didn't say anything until we got onto the highway. Then I said, "Dalton's father is a real jerk, isn't he?"

"I haven't heard that much cursing," said my dad, "since your grandmother found out *Guiding Light* had been cancelled."

"Dad," I said, "where did you learn to fight like that?"

"I didn't hit anybody!" he said.

"No, but you got all ninja warrior on Mr. Cooke when he tried to hit *you*," I said.

"Ah, that's just one of the many defensive maneuvers I learned while studying under the esteemed ninja masters in Japan," he said.

"No! For real?" I asked.

But it wasn't.

RAINY DAY BLUES

It had been raining for the past two days.

My mom and dad were out someplace, and the only one in the house besides me was Kelly.

176

I felt trapped. I couldn't ride my bike anywhere because of the rain and mud. And even if I could go someplace, like the mall, to see a movie or get something to eat, I'd have to spend money that I don't have because I'm saving every penny for that camcorder.

If I were an adult, I wouldn't have these problems. I could just get in my car and drive anyplace, even to the airport to get on a plane and fly someplace where it wasn't raining. When I got there, I could rent a car and drive to the beach and buy a hat and rent a Jet Ski and later go parasailing, then spend the night in a nice hotel that had a TV with four hundred channels and a mini-bar with twenty different kinds of candy bars.

So that's one more thing I want to add to my Ten Things I Hate about Being 14 List: I hate being fourteen. It's like my life is one big hostage situation, and I'm the hostage.

That sounds like something Kelly might say.

I was so bored that I decided to check in on Kelly and ask her if she wanted to watch a movie or bake cookies with me or something.

Her bedroom door was open, and she was on the phone. I heard her say, "I love that sort of thing! It's so romantic, even if it is on one of those phony reality shows."

She sounded like she was in a good mood, so I knocked and said, "Kelly?"

She whipped around and barked, "WHAT?!"

Suddenly, her mood wasn't looking so good anymore.

"Uh, yeah," I said, "I was wondering if you wanted to bake some cookies ...?"

"Bake some cookies?" she yelled. "Are you insane? Get out of here!"

Then she turned back to the phone and said, "Sorry, it's my stupid little brother. He wants me to bake him some cookies. Yeah, like I'm his personal chef!"

I decided not to bother explaining what I really meant to say.

As I walked back down the hall, I heard her say: "You wouldn't believe what I have to put up with around here, especially with him. It's like I'm tumbling down an endless waterslide of adolescent drivel and negative energy!"

Splash.

THE REVIEWS ARE IN

The Farkus Family Donuts commercial that I worked on was scheduled to make its debut during the six o'clock news.

My mom had called Director Sam's studio, and the girl who

answered the phone said that it was going to be shown in the first batch of commercials at the top of the hour.

My mom had prepared dinner (my favorite, baked lasagna), and we were going to be eating it in the dining room with the good dishes, because this was a special occasion.

In addition to the four of us, Freddie and his mom were there, and Miss Sadie, who was all dressed up like it was a big movie premiere or something. She even had on this big flower (a "corsage" my mom called it), which was fake, but Miss Sadie had sprayed perfume on it to make it smell real, except the perfume smelled like that stuff you squirt into the toilet to kill the stank.

I was real pumped because I knew that even if I didn't get a movie contract out of this commercial, at least I'd be the only person in my family to ever be on TV regularly—you know, the same commercial repeating over and over again until everybody's sick to death of it.

My mom was once on the TV news complaining about the airport, but that was only one time, and for only about seven seconds, so it doesn't count.

By six o'clock we were in front of the TV.

"This is so exciting," said Mrs. Schnase. "It reminds me of the time your father was on *Bowling for Bucks*. Do you remember that, Freddie?"

"Mom," said Freddie, "I wasn't even born yet when Dad was on *Bowling for Bucks*."

"Oh, that's right," said his mom.

"Diana," said Miss Sadie, "is there any garlic in that lasagna? Because, I don't know if I told you, but garlic gives me the indigestion."

"No garlic, Mrs. Grubnik," said my mom.

"We should have eaten before watching this," said Kelly, "because I'm afraid after I see Larkin on TV, I'll lose my appetite."

"Shh, everybody," I said, "the news is starting!"

We watched the news in silence, but I was so nervous that I didn't hear a word the news people were saying.

Then the news guy said, "Up next: those beautiful yet deadly flowers in your garden, and what you should know about them."

What followed was a commercial for car insurance.

I was holding my breath the whole time.

Then that lady and the ballet girl I'd seen at the studio appeared.

"THIS IS IT!" I shouted.

Then a mom at a breakfast table snatched a banana out of a boy's hand and said, "Who needs a fresh banana when you can have a Farkus Family Donut?"

Next were two police officers in a patrol car. The female officer snatched the donut out of her partner's hand and said: "Why have just any donut, when you can have a Farkus Family Donut?"

That was followed by a picture of a bunch of donuts, and a voice said, "Farkus Family Donuts now available at all Crestline Markets, Pepe's, and Super Fast Stores."

Then there was a fat guy talking about a mattress sale.

"Where were you, Larkin?" asked Freddie's mom. "I didn't see you in the commercial."

"Maybe he was in the back of the cop car," snickered Kelly, "in handcuffs."

"That's enough, Kelly," said my mom.

I couldn't say anything because I didn't know what to say.

"How about garlic powder?" asked Miss Sadie. "That upsets my stomach, too."

"There's no garlic of any kind in the lasagna," said my mom.

Finally, I said, "Maybe they made two commercials, and they're going to show the one I'm in later."

"That's unlikely, son," said my dad, "but we're recording the entire news hour, so if there is a second commercial, we'll have it."

"You mean they might have made *another* donut commercial? A cheesier one than *that* one?" said Kelly.

"What probably happened," said my dad, "is the director decided not to use the footage of you and Dalton."

"But we got paid for it, right?" I asked.

"Yes, and you can keep the money," he said, "but, Larkin, you know that directors edit out scenes all the time."

"Well, it ought to be against the law," I said, and I meant it.

"How about we all move into the dining room and have dinner?" said my mom.

"I'm not hungry," I said. "I don't feel so good."

Then I went up to my room and threw myself on my bed.

I decided that I hated Sam the Director and everyone who worked for him. I also hated everybody in my entire family, especially Kelly, and everybody at school. I also decided I hated every single person I'd ever met in my entire life.

I thought about it for a while, and decided I also hated people that I'd never met, famous successful people who made movies and were all somehow responsible for this terrible thing that had happened to me.

Oh, yeah, and Dalton Cooke.

I had almost forgotten about him.

Then I realized that Dalton was probably going through the exact same thing as me. He and his stupid family were probably still sitting in front of the TV waiting for Dalton's moronic face to appear.

And it had to be a lot worse for Dalton, because he'd spent the past two weeks telling everybody that he was going to be a big TV star. He'd told a lot more people than I did, and he'd even posted signs on the school bulletin boards and announced it over the P.A. system.

That, I knew, would make him out to be an even bigger loser than me.

And I felt good about that.

Suddenly, I didn't hate everybody so much anymore.

I went into the bathroom and washed my face, then joined my family and friends downstairs for dinner.

MISSING PIECES

While I was searching in the cabinets for some paper for the computer printer, I found the box my dad had brought home that day I'd gone with him to the office.

I opened it up and inside were some VCR tapes and reels of film, eight-millimeter movie film. Each little reel had a title written on it. Some of the titles were *Egg Up, Forgotten Promises, The Voodoo Curse,* and *Destiny with a Side of Fries.*

I looked in the cabinet and found the movie projector we'd also brought home that day. I plugged it in to see if it worked, and it did—the fan and light popped right on when I flicked the switch.

Because there didn't seem to be any flat white surfaces downstairs that would make a good projection screen, I took the projector and films up to my room and set it up on the floor. The wall next to my closet was the movie screen.

The first film I watched was *Forgotten Promises*. It didn't have any sound (none of them did), so I had to figure out what was happening from the picture alone. It seemed to be about a guy and a girl who had a fight about a dog, or maybe about a mess the dog made. Then the girl slapped the guy and ran outside. I

184

think she got run over by a car, but I wasn't too sure because everything was so dark.

At the end, she was walking in a cemetery and it was snowing. There she met a skinny priest. I got a good look at the priest and couldn't believe my eyes. I had to rewind it and look again. Yes, it was true, my dad was the priest! There he was, just a teenager, playing a priest in a movie. And it looked just like him, only a whole lot younger.

The next movie was *Egg Up,* and it was about a skinny guy, my dad again, chasing after a car until it ran over an egg.

The third movie was *Voodoo Curse,* and it showed this girl walking along, all happy and everything.

Then you see an evil girl watching her from a window. You could tell she was evil from all the makeup she was wearing. Again, I had to rewind when I realized the evil girl was my aunt Dorothy! No lie, there she was all young and thin and looking just like Aunt Dorothy, only younger and thinner.

So, anyway, Aunt Dorothy hates this other girl, and we know it because we see her thinking about strangling her. The first girl wipes her nose and drops the tissue, and after she leaves, Aunt Dorothy picks up the tissue and thinks evil thoughts.

Then Evil Aunt Dorothy goes into a room (in my Grandmom Pace's basement, I think), lights a candle, and says something to a picture of the devil. Then she takes a piece of paper with a drawing of a spider on it and balls it up with the tissue the girl had dropped, and lights it on fire.

In the last scene, you see the first girl waking up in bed covered by little plastic spiders that we're supposed to think are real, and when she screams, a spider pops out of her mouth.

At the very end of *Voodoo Curse* were credits that read: "Written and Directed by Marty Pace" and "Starring Dotty Pace and Paula Ruckert."

My dad made movies! How cool is that?

I watched every single movie in that box, and it was an awesome experience. I saw pieces of my dad's life that I never knew existed. I saw my aunts and uncle when they were kids, my grandmom when she had dark hair, and my grandpa when he was alive and walking around.

And I began to think that maybe my dad might secretly be an Accidental Genius.

He probably inherited it from me.

GETTING PERSONAL

I hadn't seen Dalton for several days after the donut commercial had aired. I figured he must've been hiding out or something.

Then on Thursday, I was walking down the hall at school and I heard him yell, "Hey, Flashy Pants."

Flashy Pants? That doesn't sound anything like Larkin Pace. I looked down at my pants, and they were totally ordinary. He must be losing it.

He was leaning against the wall. With him were Stinky, Squishy, and Brooke. "Where ya been, Dalton?" I asked. "Hiding from the paparazzi?"

"Cute," said Dalton, not meaning it. Then he yelled, "Hey, everybody, right there's the reason my acting/modeling career crashed and burned." He pointed at me. "Captain Camera here doesn't know how to ride a skateboard."

"To get from here to there, this is what he looks like on a board," said Dalton. He flung his arms up and jerked around like a drunk guy in a cartoon.

"And not only that," continued Dalton. "When his pants fell down, he started crying, 'Wah! Wah! Wah!' because the whole cast and crew got a good look at his baby boy Batman underwear."

Everybody laughed.

"X-Men," I yelled, "not Batman, and you're the one who kept messing up, you big liar!"

"You're the liar," said Dalton.

"No, *you're* lying," I said, and I got right in his face.

"What are you gonna do, Underpants Boy? Hit me?"

I was so angry that for a couple of seconds I actually considered it, but I knew if I did, he'd hit me back and it would hurt.

Then I remembered how mean Dalton's dad was to him and, well, I don't know, I sort of felt sorry for him. So I backed up and walked away.

"There he goes," yelled Dalton. "The baby's going home because he's had an accident in his superhero underpants. Maybe you should tell your mommy to put you in a diaper instead, baby."

When I got home, there was a letter addressed to me on the kitchen table. It had a stamp on it but no return address.

I opened it and when I pulled out the note that was inside, a five-dollar bill fell to the floor. I picked it up and read the note.

I read my name again. Freddie had written my name, and when I read it, in my head, I could hear him saying it.

Okay, it's kind of weird, and it's not the same as actually hearing Freddie say my name out loud, but it's a start.

MY KIND OF CHORE

I was in a bad mood when I woke up this morning.

I didn't know why I was in a bad mood and I didn't want to think about why I was in a bad mood, because if I thought about it, I might figure out why I was in a bad mood, and that would put me in an even worse mood.

It didn't help my mood when I got to the barn and heard a fight going on in the hayloft. Two cats were going at it. They weren't getting physical or anything, just making a lot of noise.

So I climbed up there, sat down, and tried to reason with them. Cats don't take to counseling too well, but after I sat with each of them, told them they were beautiful and special, they calmed down.

After I fed the rest of the animals in the barn, then the chickens, I took the Buddies for a walk in the woods. I don't know whether it was because of the fifteen wagging tails, or because of the way the woods were all dressed up like summer, but I started to feel a little better about things. Just a little.

When we got back, I fed the Buddies and hosed off a couple of rowdy Buds who'd taken a dip the duck pond. Then I climbed onto the roof of the shed and just sat there for a while.

I mostly thought about the future, and in particular, this summer. It was coming soon—Thursday was the last day of school—and it would be my first summer without Brooke. No more snarking on people at the mall or doing movie scenes at the lake or just talking to her about stuff.

I felt bad. Real bad. Without Brooke in my life, it was like, I don't know, I'd lost the other half of my rainbow.

And then there was the money issue. For what I was getting paid to work once a week for Miss Sadie, it would be a long time before I'd be able to buy the camcorder of my dreams.

Sometimes life really is one big deflated jump house punctured by the slings and arrows of unrealistic expectations and imitation chocolate syrup, or whatever it was Kelly had said last night at dinner when she didn't like the dessert.

All that worrying had made me hungry, so I headed to breakfast.

My dad was in the kitchen, and on the table was the box of eight-millimeter films I had secretly watched. I hadn't told him that I'd seen them, because I thought he's get mad at me for snooping through his personal stuff.

On the table was another box. It was a smaller one, and it contained all our family photos and assorted home movies on DVDs and VHS tapes. That box has always been stored in the closet under the stairs, and we'd all looked through it a million times, so I knew I wouldn't get into trouble for recognizing it.

"Hey, Dad," I said. "What's up?"

"Larkin," he said, "I have a project that might interest you."

He explained that, in his effort to get better organized, he'd been getting prices from professionals about converting the family photos and movies to CDs and DVDs.

"And," he continued, "I thought, why should I pay some stranger to put together a video version of our family's life, when I have someone living right here who has the talent to do the exact same thing, and in addition, has a personal interest in it?"

"Who?" I said.

"You!" said my dad.

"Oh," I said, "but I don't know how to convert eight-millimeter film strips to DVD."

"Who said anything about eight-millimeter films?" he asked.

Uh-oh, I was busted.

"Well," I confessed, "I sort of looked at your eight-millimeter movies from high school and I thought they were really cool, especially the one with Aunt Dorothy putting a voodoo curse on the girl in the short, short pants, and I'm very sorry I messed with your personal stuff."

"That's okay," said my dad. "I *figured* it was you who'd left the film reel on the projector when you put it away."

Oops.

"There's a low-tech method of converting film to DVD," he said. "You film the image with your digital camera as it's projected on the screen. Then you can edit it in the computer and add a sound track later."

"Just like a bootlegger filming a movie in a theater!" I said. "Except we'll be bootlegging our own movies. I mean, *your* own movies."

"That's fine with me," said my dad. "And I'm thinking you could do the whole job for, let's say . . . eight hundred dollars?"

"Are you kidding?" I said.

"That's not enough?" he asked. "The guy at Todd's Video

Connection said he'd do it for seven fifty, but he had a rather bad attitude and—"

"Are you kidding? YES! YES! YES! I'll do it! Eight hundred dollars!" I shouted. I ran around the table a couple of times, hugged my dad, and kissed him on the face. Then I grabbed a frozen waffle, ran out the door, and yelled at the Buddies, "Back to the woods!"

They charged after me, and we spent the rest of the morning and a good part of the afternoon thrashing about out there and whooping it up.

I even jumped in the duck pond a few times.

SCHOOL'S OUT

Okay, this just happened, so I'm writing it down right now. It'll be my last post in this blog.

I was in the quad looking for Freddie, because he'd left his hat in the cafeteria and I wanted to give it to him. Just then, Brooke came up to me and told me that she knows that all that stuff Dalton was saying about how I screwed up the donut commercial wasn't true.

"Why?" I said. "Did he tell you what really happened?"

"No," she said. "It's because I know him and I know you and I know who's telling the truth."

I felt a little better.

Then she told me how much she loves Stella, and what a great dog she is, but she thinks Stella misses being with the Buddies. So, could she, like, bring Stella to the farm for a visit, maybe on Sunday, and we could hang out together?

I'm like, "Yeaaaah." And I thought to myself, hey, this might not be such a bad summer after all.

As she started to walk away, she turned and said, "Nothing succeeds like excess. You should know that, Tony."

It was from *Scarface*.

"Oh, yeah?" I said. "Would you kiss me if I wore the hat?" I put on Freddie's hat.

She moved up close to me, like she was going to tell me a secret, and whispered, "No."

Then she kissed me on the cheek and went down the steps.

I watched Dalton take her hand, and the two of them walked away.

I took a deep breath and said to myself, "Well, at least they're not doing the Love Dance."

LARKIN PACE'S READING GROUP GUIDE

1. Early in the book, Larkin lists the ten things that bug him about his dad, and ten things that bother him about his sister, Kelly. List some of the things that bother you about certain members of your own family. Also, what do you find amusing about some of your family members? For example, my dad always says, "Ahh, that felt good. I ought to do that more often," every time he comes out of the bathroom after having made a deposit. My sister finds that annoying, but I find it very amusing.

2. Larkin describes his sister Kelly as a "total thug," and complains that she always gets her way. Kelly gripes that Larkin is the one their parents favor. Who's right? Name a few of Kelly's nicer qualities. Give yourself some time. Try harder.

3. Larkin dislikes the high-fiber cereal his mom buys, saying it tastes like "critter kibble." What is critter kibble? What are your favorite breakfast cereals? What's the grossest pizza topping you ever ate, or almost ate? Would you eat a pizza with pineapple on it? Raisins? M&M's?

4. As they are leaving the skating rink, Brooke implies that she doesn't consider herself to be Larkin's girlfriend. A surprised Larkin can't figure out how to respond to her, and so he clams up and says nothing. Later he thinks he should have acted all macho and given her a big, sexy kiss. Do you think that method would have worked? What do you think he could have said or done to change her mind? Something short of creating a hostage situation, that is.

5. Kelly names her cat Pandora, which is the name of a mythical Greek woman who opened a box that unleashed a world of hurt. Do you know any interesting or funny cat names? For example: Dizzy, Tumbles, Cheeser, Destructo, Wasabi, Space Cadet, Catzilla . . .

6. Larkin describes Bethany Weaver's breath as smelling like sheet spit. Explain sheet spit. What's a nice way of telling someone their breath stinks? What's a not so nice way?

7. While waiting for the ghost cat to make an appearance, Larkin mentions three scary movies: *The Shining*, *The Blair Witch Project*, and *Paranormal Activity*. What's the scariest horror movie you've ever seen? What's the scariest non-horror movie you've ever seen, other than *The Sound of Music*?

8. When he goes to lunch with Drew Carey, Larkin orders the fanciest meal he can think of: shrimp cocktail, filet mignon, and Caesar salad. If someone were paying for your dinner at an expensive restaurant, and you could order anything you wanted, what would it be? Note: not on the menu are PB&J sandwiches, fries, or breakfast cereal.

9. Mr. Bivic, Larkin's French teacher, has an interesting way of turning a phrase. For example: "Before you leap, you should look what is on your feet." What do you think he meant to say by that? Can you translate the following Bivications? "Every picture has big ears." "There's no time like the gift that keeps on giving." And "Two wrongs don't make the customer always right."

10. When Larkin realizes his scene had been cut from the TV commercial, he gets all sad and moody. Then, when he realizes that Dalton is probably experiencing the same feelings, he feels a lot better. When you're feeling a bit down, what can usually cheer you up? Your favorite pet? Finding a ten-dollar bill in your jacket pocket? Chocolate?

"REGULAR RUSSELL" SHOWBOATS AT THE ICE RINK.

IN A DELETED SCENE, A SHORT CIRCUIT CAUSES
FREDDIE'S SOMBRERO TO IGNITE ON HAT DAY.

IN A DELETED BOWLING SEQUENCE, BROOKE AND
LARKIN DO A SCENE FROM THE MOVIE "SURF'S UP."

THE ILLUSTRATION THAT WAS CUT FROM PAGE 116.

LARKIN HIDES UNDER THE STAIRS AFTER THE "VENDETTA" INCIDENT AT THE SCHOOL DANCE.

ON PAGE 157, LARKIN SETS OUT TO HELP A LOST DOG, LEAVING THE KEY IN THE IGNITION OF HIS MOM'S TRUCK.

LARKIN'S "GHOST CAT" PRACTICAL JOKE ON FREDDIE
MISFIRES AND GETS MRS. SCHNASE INSTEAD.

INSTEAD OF "SCARFACE", LARKIN AND BROOKE ORIGINALLY PERFORMED A SCENE FROM "ADDAMS FAMILY VALUES" ON THE LAST DAY OF SCHOOL.